THE ARCANE QUEST

ANDREW S. FRENCH

NEONOIR BOOKS

The Arcane Supernatural Thriller Series

Book one: The Arcane

Book two: The Arcane Identity

Book three: The Arcane Quest

Book four: The Arcane Ultimatum

The Ella Finn Fantasy Novella Series

Ella and the Elementals

Ella and the Multiverse

Ella and the Monsters

Ella and the Dreamers

Supernatural Short Stories

Dead Souls

The Shadow

Science Fiction

The Time Traveller's Murder

The Mercy Sleep

Bodies

The Astrid Snow series

Book one: Don't Fear the Reaper

Book two: The Killing Moon

Book three: Lost in America

Book four: Gone to Texas

Book five: The Final Girl

The Detective Jen Flowers series

Book one: The Hashtag Killer

Book two: Serial Killer

Book three: Night Killer

Book four: The Killer Inside Them

Northern Crime Fiction

Where The Bodies Are Buried

The Ophelia Red series

Book one: Ophelia Red

Crime Short Stories

Call Me: An Astrid Snow Short Story

Dark Snow: An Astrid Snow Short Story

Bette Davis Eyes: Detective Flowers Short Story

Go to www.andrewsfrench.com for more information.

1 ALICE: IN THE SHADOWS

I t was cold at four o'clock in the morning when evil laughed at me.

A six-foot-tall bloke built for Wrestle Mania probably wasn't too afraid when he saw a teenage girl breaking into the house he protected. I stumbled past the rubbish on the floor and ignored the smell of stale pizza and cider in the room. Then I wiped the sweat from my top lip and spoke to him.

'Did I interrupt your party?'

His grin grew darker and covered his face, most of which appeared to have been borrowed from a failed boxer.

'It looks like it's just about to get started, girlie.'

I left the weapons inside my jacket. 'I'm not here for you. If you tell me what I want, I'll let you go.'

He crushed the can in his hand and dropped it to the floor. Then he removed the large knife from the back of his trousers.

'I'm going to cut you a little before giving you to the others.'

Then he approached me with the blade glistening in his

fingers. Perhaps he wanted to keep me as food for the monsters he was there to protect, or maybe he thought he'd have some fun with the teenage girl invading his environment. But experience had taught me there would be nothing enjoyable about being there.

And I was prepared for anything he did. Which meant when he attempted to grab my hand, it was easy to dodge his lunge, stepping to the side and away from the end of the knife.

But that's when I made a mistake.

Perhaps it was the lack of sleep I'd had the last two days or the result of my arrogance. Or maybe it was the constant worry I had for my sister Cassie and my mother, Mary. Both of them had been taken from me, which was why I was in that house in the early hours of the morning.

Whatever the reason, the mistake came and I didn't look at where I was stepping as I dodged the protector of monsters. My shoes were already wet from the constant rain I'd trudged through to get there, so when my foot landed on an empty cider can, there was nothing I could do but slip and fall onto the dirty carpet.

My shoulder hit the wall as my knee buckled. I grimaced as I rolled through the rubbish and reached the sofa on the other side of the room. He laughed and waved the knife in front of him.

'You broke into the wrong house, kid.'

He sprang towards me and there was no time to reach for a weapon inside my jacket. Instead, I grabbed a thick piece of discarded pizza and hurled it at him. I'd never been good at sports or throwing things before I'd discovered my identical twin sister, but now my aim was straight and true, going for his face as a distraction. Then I'd be able to get up and meet him square on.

Unfortunately for him, he twisted his head slightly, and the pizza struck him in the middle of his eye. The crust must have been harder than I thought because he dropped to the floor instantly.

I jumped up before he could recover, but I didn't need to worry. As I inched towards him and peered at his face, it was clear the slice had gone through his pupil and pierced his brain.

There was no remorse in me as I dragged the body across the carpet and placed his corpse next to the door. Those I'd come for would find it difficult getting in with him there, giving me plenty of time to be ready. I checked the rest of the room to ensure it was clear of any more danger, and then settled into the sofa. I opened the internet on my phone and waited for the sun to come up. The monsters would have all slithered back by then.

I ignored the smell and calmed my beating heart. It had been a frustrating week since the Queen of Lies had tricked my sister and me, trapping Cassie in America and attempting to abduct me. We'd saved the world from nuclear Armageddon, but it was the only positive thing to come out of the experience. Now the police hunted me for murders I hadn't committed, and I had no transport or money to help me in my quest for Cassie and my mother.

Therefore, my frustration had forced me to hunt monsters and find the vampire who had my mother. Dracula was out of my range, but his children weren't, for who else could tell me where the Lord of the Undead was but those who followed him? Heading away from London, I'd found two other groups of vamps while searching for information on Dracula's whereabouts, but both had proved useless.

And now I was in this nest.

I shook the smell of vampires from my mind and trawled through the morning's social media posts, looking fruitlessly for any mention of Cassie. Lucy, the Devil herself, claimed the Americans had captured my sister and were holding her hostage, but could I believe what she'd said? I had little choice and knew I needed my mother's help before we could all be reunited as a family again.

So I sat there and waited.

It was thirty minutes before the noise crept through the house.

I removed the weapons from my jacket and placed one on each of my legs. The banging on the door was the first sign the occupants had returned. It didn't take them long to push it open and force the corpse from it.

I sat ten feet from them. They came through one by one, climbed over the body without a second glance at the dead man, and lined up opposite me: six vampires in a row peering at the intruder in their lair. I'd expected more of them. If this were a movie, they'd all be dressed in black and showing off long fingernails and yellowing teeth, hissing at me. Yet, this bunch looked like they'd stepped out of a meeting with a group of accountants: four men and two women, all wearing suits, all perfectly groomed, with soulless eyes fixed on me. Maybe they weren't vampires but bankers or lawyers.

The tallest moved forward and flashed his fangs at me.

'Did someone order takeaway?'

The gang laughed as one, the sound of thunder and lightning cracking through teeth sharpened to within an inch of their lives. Or perhaps it would be to an inch of mine. The tall one stepped closer, with most of his face obscured by a ragged red beard and long ruby-hewed hair, so he resembled a failed drummer from some desperate grunge band.

'We know how much you like chicken, Marv?'

Again, they erupted into hilarity with those words from the willowy young woman ready to offer someone a bank loan. She tilted her head to one side, more interested in her friend's reaction than mine. The tall red-headed man, Marv, met my gaze and didn't turn away.

'Who cut your hair, girl? You look like a gothic crow.'

'If you tell me what I want, I won't have to kill you all.'

The vampire gang turned to each other before bursting into more frenzied amusement. The woman strode next to Marv.

'Can we keep her for a while? She looks much more fun than those townies we've got downstairs.'

My heart sank. They had victims here. I couldn't let the vampires live now, no matter what I'd promise them to get what I needed.

Marv turned to the girl. 'You always want the best meat for yourself, don't you, Maddy?'

Sobbing came from behind them as they devoured me with their eyes. As the crying increased, I saw the chain in Maddy's hand. She pulled on it, and her captive jerked forward.

Then Maddy grinned at me. 'We can add her to the other snacks, though there's not much meat on her.'

I stared at the girl they'd enslaved. She wasn't a lot younger than me, maybe fourteen years old, wearing a tattered Ramones shirt and blue jeans. Dust covered her long, dark hair, and she sneezed, her eyes flickering with a yearning for release.

'Let the kid and the rest go, and I might let you live.'

It was easy to lie now, especially when faced with such

monsters.

The vampire bit her top lip and I watched her lick the blood from it.

'I'm looking forward to playing with you.' She pulled on the chain and the teenage girl grimaced. 'You'll be much more fun than the others.'

She laughed, and the rest of them joined in.

I ignored their enjoyment. 'Tell me where Dracula is, and you can go free.'

It was easy to deceive them because I'd learnt from the best. Their mirth disappeared as quickly as it had come. Panic consumed their faces as they moved back from me.

All except for Marv.

'We don't speak that name here; no vampire will say it again.'

'I don't care about your petty squabbles. Tell me what you know, or this will be the last thing you'll see.' I nodded at the stakes resting on my legs. If only I could use the Arcane abilities Lucy had blocked inside me. Or had I dreamt those like I'd dreamt of a life at university and a career as a scientist?

No, for a moment, those gifts were real; still there but diminished. Just as quickly as they'd materialised in that field outside the prime minister's war room, now they were nearly gone. I could turn invisible for thirty seconds at the most, while teleporting left me physically sick for hours after. Flying was too dangerous. When I'd tried it last, I'd floated above the clouds, unable to move in any direction but up, only returning to earth when I was desperate and teleported to the ground. I'd suffered for a long time after that.

Reading other people's thoughts brought on a pneumatic headache and blood pouring from my nose and mouth, the same with my telekinetic powers. If I used any of them with these vamps, there was no telling what physical and mental state I'd end up in. They could pick me off if I weren't careful. Not forgetting I'd tried to use them before entering the house, and they hadn't worked.

'Why do you seek the betrayer of all vampires?' Marv's eyes were a mixture of yellow and red.

I saw no point in keeping secrets from them. 'He's imprisoned my mother.'

Those words set the others into frenzied whispers before the willowy woman spoke into Marv's ear. He peered at me.

'You and your family are the ones to blame for his treachery?'

'What do you mean?' I didn't care, but it was good to keep him talking while I considered my options.

'Not only has the deceitful one abandoned all his children, but he also strikes down any he sees, and all because of this female he loves.' He stretched out his hands as his fingers grew longer and sharper. 'It will give me great pleasure to make her daughter suffer for what she's caused.'

They lined up against me, the desperation to consume me clear in their eyes. Their anger fuelled mine.

'My mother is no human; she's the last of the Nephilim, and I'm a Child of the Arcane.'

I spoke with such authority, pride and confidence, but I still didn't understand what those words meant for me. At least they had the desired result on the vampires. All but Marv gasped and raised those dangerous nails to their faces. Beneath me, people wailed.

Marv was the only calm one. 'Which twin are you?'

'I'm Alice Arcane.'

'Is it true what they say about you?'

I removed both stakes from my legs, rolling them against each other as if ready to start a fire.

'What have you heard?'

The air was sweet as a chill slipped into the room. The weeping below ceased. I should have checked the place before the vamps had returned. I wouldn't let those people die because of my quest, because of my mistakes. Not again. My errors had lost me my sister and mother.

Marv contorted his lips into an awkward toothy smile, the points on his front teeth glistening in the gloom.

'They say you and your twin are the destroyers of worlds.' His grin grew as wide as the Grand Canyon. 'But they also say she's dead, so if that can happen to her, I'm sure it can happen to you.'

Narrow fingers clutched at my heart. Was it true, had Cassie died in America?

No, I'd have known if that was true. Our connection was growing when Lucy had separated us across the world, divided us, lied to us, and then betrayed us. But I'd know if Cassie was dead.

I stared at each vampire, deciding which one would have the knowledge I needed. Marv was the obvious choice, but he was also the most dangerous. I couldn't wait for their attack, but how would I disable them without my missing abilities?

I'd use my charm instead.

'If that's true, then the only thing I have left to live for is discovering where Dracula has my mother. If you tell me where he is, I promise to kill him for you.'

Maddy laughed at me. 'I'm going to keep your head with me after I bite it off.'

So much for the charm.

I sighed. 'We might as well get this over with then.'

2 CASSIE: PRISON

I t's hard to get lost when you don't know where you are. But I'd lost all sense of time, unaware of what part of the day it was. The temptation was to stay in bed, but I had to move. I couldn't lie there any longer.

The room was hot enough to boil an egg on the floor. They'd been alternating between increasing and decreasing the temperature, and now I was inside a sauna. The heat didn't help with the smell of last night's baked beans festering in the sink.

A rush started in my toes and surged up through me. Thousands of tiny bubbles of frustration and desperation sped through my veins, leaving my body feeling like a bottle of Coke ready to explode. Then I threw up great chunks of food and terrible coffee. That's what I blamed for my condition: that and the thing whispering at the back of my mind.

Apart from that, everything was fine, considering I was locked up.

Before that, I remembered stumbling out of a fancy American mansion with the aroma of death covering me. I was sixteen years old, but knew enough to wipe the blood from my hands.

But it wasn't enough.

I took my usual look around the cell, expecting things to be different, but they weren't. There was a comfortable bed, decent toilet and even a shower. I was fed three times a day and provided with fresh clothes regularly. If it weren't for the fact I didn't know where I was, it wouldn't be a lousy prison. And it was annoying having nothing to read. Not one guard had spoken to me since I'd woke in here the first time. Counting the meals, twenty-one so far, meant I'd been inside these four walls for at least a week.

People I never saw delivered the provisions through a small hatch. There had to be an entrance into the cell, but I couldn't see it in the pure whiteness surrounding me. The shower had an access point for ventilation, which was the only way I could think of getting out.

A door slid open in the wall. A tall woman strode in, and as the exit closed behind her, I memorised that spot on the wall. Then I wondered how much damage I could do to her with the plastic spoon from last night's meal. She pulled the chair from the corner of the room and sat opposite me.

She must have been in her mid-thirties; bright, intelligent sea-blue eyes centred inside perfect brown skin and sculptured hair, which looked like it wouldn't move in a gale-force wind. Her immaculate suit was as white as the walls. There was an iPad in her hands, humming the low sound of static electricity.

She stared at me.

'My name is Dr Olivia Erasmus.' She glanced at the computer. 'And who are you?' I remained silent, happy to let her talk. 'We've run your face through facial recognition databases and got nothing; same for your fingerprints, dental records, blood type, and DNA. You're an enigma we're finding difficult to crack.' And I wouldn't help them. 'But we have this as a starting point.'

She turned the iPad towards me and played the video. It was strange to see myself in that bunker again. When it happened, me teleporting inside and killing the president and his people, it seemed to take forever, but now, watching it on the screen, it was over in a flash. Well, it was over in the time I had to stop him from starting a nuclear war.

'I've seen better shows.' The smell of beans irritated my senses.

'The media don't know what happened in that bunker, even though some of my colleagues would like them to have the truth, beyond it was a massacre. The rumours immediately blamed the Chinese, but I can't see you working for them.' She stared at me. 'I don't think you're with any of our enemies, not the Russians or North Koreans, nor any middle-Eastern States.' Erasmus paused. 'Some of my superiors have suggested you might be a lone internal terrorist, but I believe you're something different.'

She leant in so I smelt her perfume, an overwhelming aroma of sweet lemon. Then she reached into her jacket for a cigarette and a lighter. When she lit up and blew a circle of smoke above my head, it was the final straw.

'You can't do that here; it's against my human rights.'

The foul gas staggered up to my nose and into my mouth. I scratched at my throat and coughed all over her, but she didn't flinch.

'You have no rights and you aren't human.'

I moved from her, glancing up at the invisible cameras I knew were in the walls. They weren't invisible, only hidden, but the thought made me remember the abilities I'd used when attacking the president and his supernatural entourage. Invisibility, flight, teleportation, telekinesis, and telepathy were mine for a brief period. I'd tried to recreate each of them again since my imprisonment, but to no avail.

Now, as Erasmus blew smoke my way, I gave them another go. I imagined internal fingers squeezing my brain and attempted to read her mind, but got nothing. I pictured Alice and me in Whitby and willed myself there, closing my eyes and burying my hands into my legs. I visualised the cliffs and the Abbey, recalled Kai and the Impossible Palace, and smelt the aroma of the sea with fish and chips. There was sand under my toes, saltwater on my skin.

When I opened my eyes, Erasmus dragged on her poison stick. I glared at her and decided I had no choice but to talk. She'd mentioned her superiors, so perhaps I could wrangle some useful information from her.

'You have no right to imprison me here; who are you people?' The end of her cigarette fizzled, the flame flickering like my heartbeat. 'I'm a British citizen. I demand to see my ambassador.'

Erasmus blew more smoke around the room.

'You're in no position to make demands, and I think whoever or whatever your ambassador is, they're likely to deny all knowledge of you considering what you did.'

I squeezed my eyes into their smallest point and turned my nose up at her. And not just because of the smell.

'I don't know what you're on about.' I went to the sink, bent to it and drank from the tap; the water was cold as it slithered between my lips. My back was to her as I spoke. 'I was in a field with some mates, having a party, and I must have passed out. The next thing I know, I wake up here and I'm locked away.' I faced her. 'I know you Yanks are heavy-handed with authority, but don't you think it's a bit much to lock up a kid for having a few drinks and some medicinal ciggies.' I resisted the temptation to grab her cigarette and stick it up her nose, although I considered how long it would take the security to appear and drag me off her.

She crossed her legs and scrutinised me. 'If that's the case, why don't you tell me your name?'

I wiped my mouth and sat on the bed. 'I'm Lulu.'

Erasmus nearly choked on her cigarette. The end of it caught in her teeth as she sprayed laughter at me.

'You're a fan of old black-and-white movies?'

I sat crossed-legged. 'My mum loved silent films.'

Erasmus removed a notebook from her pocket. 'And what's your mother's name?'

The question hit me with a jolt, a surge of electricity bursting through my stomach and engulfing my heart. My mother was Mary Arcane, and she'd been traded like a throwaway woman from one monster to another. I wondered what this doctor would think if I told her that. Instead, I lied.

'My mother's dead. My father disappeared before I was born.' He'd abandoned Alice and me to the archangels; betrayed our mother and us. The anger growing in me, what I felt for him, transferred to Erasmus. 'So, I'm an orphan, really, but when I get out of here, I'll sue the crap out of you and whoever it is you work for.'

I jumped from the bed and leant over her, my face pushed so far into hers we were nearly joined at the nose. Nothing stirred between us as I waited for the guards to burst in and drag me away. But nothing happened or moved, apart from the slight upturn of her lips as she smiled at me.

'You're a terrible liar, Lulu. You make a much better assassin.'

My legs trembled as I stumbled back to the bed. The

bile rose again in my gut, but I forced it down and tasted the remains of last night's food.

I dug my nails into the sheets.

'I've no idea what you're talking about. That's not me in that video, just some lookalike. I mean, how could a sixteen-year-old kid do all those things and kill all those people? She's flying and jumping around in that clip like a ninja-superhero; it's probably all fake, anyway.' I glared at her. 'You should get me a lawyer.'

Her grin grew wider. She opened a notebook and flicked through the pages.

'Okay, we'll come to your true name, eventually. But, first, you need to realise your assassination of the President of the United States and the murder of at least a dozen others has changed the world completely. Would you like to know how?'

I guessed my bluff hadn't worked on her. 'What do you mean?'

'You've started a new Cold War which could turn into a hot one easily.' I watched as she spoke, wondering if I could take her hostage as a way out of this place. 'Your attack and what happened in the UK changed the whole dynamic of global politics.' She placed the notebook on her knee. 'Apparently, and this came as a shock to me when I was informed, a select minority in certain countries have always known supernatural creatures exist yet kept it quiet because they believed they weren't a threat to governments and world leaders. But that's all different now, thanks to you. America and other western powers are focusing on the supernatural, but there's a split in how it should be handled. One faction perceives them as an evil that should be destroyed, the other side wanting to keep them hidden from the public and use their abilities. So there's a scramble going on. You might call it a supernatural arms race between states, and a conflict between those trying to keep the likes of you secret from the public and those who want to control or kill you.'

Erasmus picked up her notebook and waited for me to speak. Was there any point in me continuing to deny what I'd done, to refute what I was?

'It's a fascinating story, Dr Erasmus, but I told you I was only having a party in your country, and that was it. I know nothing about this other stuff you said.'

She slid the notebook into her pocket and leant close to me, her voice just above a whisper.

'Some people I work for are champing at the bit to get in here and cut you open to see what makes you tick; they're keen to experiment on you while you're awake to discover what you are. Others want to torture and kill you for what you did to the president, but I'm here to help you.' She placed her hand on me, and I didn't flinch. 'I don't believe you were inside the presidential bunker as an assassin. I think you were there to stop the end of the world: you were there to save us all.' She paused, waiting for me to process that information. 'Now I need you to save us again.'

3 ALICE: RELEASE THE BATS

The only sound in the room was the young girl sobbing. I stared at the group and waited. Experience had taught me that vampires, even in groups like this, were essentially loners. They weren't like werewolves who tended to attack as a pack, instead resembling reality TV contestants desperate to show off to everyone else.

From examining the leader, I could tell he wouldn't be rushing into battle first, leaving his goons to do all the hard work. Maddy was clinging to her captive, so I didn't expect her to attack me straight away.

That left four of them.

The other female vamp looked older, in her late fifties with scruffy brown hair and broken eyes. The vampire next to her was smaller and thinner, scowling like a coiled spring ready to jump. The other two were identical twins, bald as eggs and looking twice as hard-boiled.

Like Marv and Maddy, the other men must have thought I was beneath them as they let the older woman reach for me as I sat.

However, I was quicker than her, moving off the sofa

and getting behind her. I got my arm around her throat and pulled her into me, a stake pointed at her neck. Every vamp I'd met before had been quick and strong, but I knew it all depended on when they'd fed.

And they all looked hungry as I spoke to Marv.

'Tell me what I want and let the humans go, and I won't hurt her.'

He shook his head. 'I don't care what happens to her. There's plenty more where she came from.'

Was he bluffing? It didn't matter if I was ready to slay the vampire to get what I wanted and free the victims. And hadn't I gone there to kill the monsters once I'd got what I needed?

Yes, but not like this. I couldn't murder her when she had her back to me. She was the monster, not me.

I gripped the stake close to her throat before pushing her into them. The older vamp fell into the others, and they staggered backwards. Maddy pulled on the chain of her victim while Marv picked at his teeth. I probably should have killed the female vampire when it was easy, but I wasn't that ruthless. I'm sure Cassie would have. That thought made my heart ache and distracted me from what came next.

The bald twins rushed me together, with fangs bared and aiming straight for my throat. The stake in my right hand smashed into the jaw of the closer one, knocking him into his brother and both of them over the coffee table in the middle of the room. They rolled over the floor, scattering beer cans everywhere, as I leant forward with the stakes aimed towards their throats.

Before I could connect with either of them, the skinny vampire leapt on to my back and grabbed my head. I thrust up to shake him off, but it was no use as he gripped on tight.

I twisted around the room like a spinning top, trying to get rid of him. He dug his nails into my skin and clung on, his legs flailing from side to side and smacking into the older woman as she ran at me. She went flying into a big-screen TV, and glass shattered everywhere.

Then I threw myself into the wall and squashed the attacker on my back into it. He groaned before slipping off me. I wiped the blood from my face and stared at Marv and Maddy. They continued to grin as if this was an everyday occurrence.

I rested my hand on the bookcase next to me to steady my legs. That's when I realised the blood on my lips wasn't mine. It had slithered into my mouth and down my throat before I could spit it to the floor. It tasted like lousy vinegar and I nearly choked on it. I was about to gag when I heard children crying somewhere in the house. Every part of me throbbed, and I wondered if I'd overestimated my abilities on coming here.

Marv must have seen the doubt in my eyes as he shook his head at me.

'You're no more of the Arcane than I am, girl.' He stroked the hair of the kid Maddy had in chains. 'And now we'll finish you off together.'

Before I could move, all six of them were on me, dragging me into the carpet and the rubbish at my feet. The stink of stale pizza and old alcohol rushed up my nose as a vamp bit my hand. I tried to scream, but undead fingers found my mouth and forced their way between my lips. I clamped down on them, taking a chunk of vampire flesh and blood and swallowing it in one go.

Then Maddy whispered into my ear, 'I'm going to enjoy this, but I'll take my time.'

She pressed her teeth next to my throat as one of the

others clawed their nails through my trousers and across my leg.

How could I have been so stupid as to come here unprepared and without rest?

I closed my eyes and pictured Cassie and my mother while I waited for the inevitable.

Then it happened.

I teleported in an instant, out from underneath them and hovering above the pile. Then I plunged both stakes into the neck of the skinny vamp on the top. He howled as I whipped the wood out and fell, rolling off him and the others. I was up in one movement, watching him thrash around in the pizza boxes and beer cans while I scanned the room. Marv, Maddy and the chained girl weren't there, just the other three monsters readying to attack me again.

My brain felt as if it was underwater as they lunged at me together. I turned invisible and teleported at the same time. It was only a few feet away as I reappeared into the bookcase and sent books all over the carpet. The noise was enough for the vamps to snap their heads towards me.

But it was too late for them. My arms whirled through the air like the sails of a demented windmill, and I shoved blood-stained wood into their necks, one after the other, just as I turned visible again.

As they crashed to the floor in a wail of screams, I stumbled into the far wall and gathered my bearings. My Arcane abilities had returned at the right time, somehow, but using them had taken a painful toll on me: my head throbbed as if it was inside a nuclear power plant, while it was taking all of my self-control to stop my legs from collapsing underneath me.

My vision blurred as I heard the footsteps behind me.

I threw up as I twisted around and stabbed Marv in

both legs. Blood seeped out of him as he staggered into a table and sent plates and cups flying. The other vampires grasped at each other, the blood spurting from them like monstrous geysers.

'No!' Marv shouted as I fell into him. I pushed him onto the table as it broke, with splintered wood crashing to the floor. My legs pinned him to the ground as his life leaked over me.

The blade was on his throat as I spoke. 'You've got one last chance, Marv.'

Blood gurgled out of his lips as he struggled to talk.

'Will you... will you spare me?'

'I promise.' The lies became easier the more I said them. I relaxed my grip, but not enough for him to toss me aside.

'Then, I'll help you.' The guarantee of life sparkled inside his lifeless eyes. 'The betrayer of all vampires has a sister, but no one has seen her since the 1940s. It's rumoured he imprisoned her somewhere in London during the Second World War.'

At last, after fruitless searching and endless dead vamps, here was something that might help.

'Does this sister have a name?' The irony of having to locate Dracula's sibling to find mine wasn't lost on me.

'No one knows. All we hear are rumours of someone who betrayed him years ago.' He swallowed blood as he spoke. 'They mention the name Isabella in whispers. That's all I can tell you.'

I stood off him, eyes fixed on his face. 'That'll do.'

I swiped the knife through his neck as he smiled, cutting away as I thought of the victims these monsters had downstairs. His head tumbled to one side as I scanned the room. Somebody else could clean up this mess. No doubt the police would put this down to gang violence or a random psychopath.

Marv's skull rolled across the floor as I threw up again, my guts spewing out what little food I'd had the last two days. I wiped my mouth and considered his words. Could it be true what he'd said about Isabella? And would Isabella be the Bella I'd met at the Nexus on Lindisfarne? It hardly seemed possible. That maniac Dr Rivers claimed they didn't know their imprisoned vampire's name and had only named her after the old movie actor Bela Lugosi. Perhaps that was another of her lies.

As all those things rattled inside my head, a slow hand-clap came from the entrance to the room. I peered up to see Maddy there, still holding the chain and her captive.

'I didn't think you had it in you.' She pulled the girl closer to her, placing one hand around the teenager's neck. 'I mean, no offence, but you're not much to look at.' She gazed at me. 'How did you do all those tricks?'

'Does it matter?' I gathered what strength I had and stood as tall as I could. 'Because I can use them again to kill you.'

Maddy used her nail to draw blood across the girl's skin. 'Can you do your magic before I slit her throat? Are even you that quick?'

Was I? I didn't think so, not in my present state. I had no idea why they'd reappeared, so there was no guarantee my abilities were still there.

I glanced at the dead vampires around me. 'I guess you want revenge for them.'

She laughed like a teenager on prom night. 'God, no. You did me a favour in getting rid of them. I'd been wondering how I was going to do it, and then you turned up.' She rattled the chain and gave me a mock curtsy. 'And because of that, I'll let you and the others live.'

Before I could reply, she was out of the door, leaving the scared girl shivering in the doorway. I stumbled to her as she fell, catching her and holding her up. She grabbed me around the waist, clutching on for eternity. Then I prised her arms from me and settled her on the sofa.

'Where are the others?' I said.

She raised a pale hand to wipe the tears from her cheeks. 'Downstairs.'

I stood and used my foot to push a body out of the way and opened the door.

There were stairs on the right, unnoticed before in my enthusiasm to interrogate the vampires. I strode down and listened for those sobs. There was a door at the end. It was unlocked, and I stepped through. There was no light switch, so I removed my mobile and turned on the torch.

It took twenty minutes to get the group of four children unchained and out of the building. As I left, I liberated Marv's phone from his useless body, confident in the fact he wouldn't need it anymore. I gave it to the girl who Maddy had chained and told her to call the police.

'Tell them whatever you want. But leave me out of it.' Let the cops believe the dead vampires were a bunch of psychopaths or child killers.

The girl took the phone from me as I started to leave. 'I know who you are,' she said.

I stopped and stared at her. 'Who do you think I am?'

The other kids stood by her side and gazed at me with admiration and relief.

'You're Alice Valentine. The cops claim you killed some kid in a park last month. We should tell them you saved us.'

I looked at the other kids, the eldest maybe a few years younger than me, but I suddenly felt older than time.

'And what will you say I saved you from?'

Their faces were ashen, their eyes wide and shimmering. I turned and walked away from them.

'You saved us from death,' the girl shouted at me.

I'd got what I wanted, and I had saved them. Now I had to continue the search for Cassie and my mother.

But I had no idea how I'd get to Lindisfarne.

And every organ in my body felt as if it was about to explode.

4 CASSIE: ERASMUS

I let her words linger in the space between us, gazing into her eyes and scrutinising her expression. I pushed my back into the concrete as I lifted a hand to my forehead to try the telepathy one more time. I focused on her face to get my mind into hers, to read if this was a trick, but it was fruitless.

So I responded to her statement instead.

'How can I save you?'

Erasmus got up from the chair, twisted her head to the side, and stared at the corner of the room for twenty seconds before returning her attention to me.

'Your life hangs by a thread while you're here. What you say and do will influence your chance of freedom, and if you'll live.' Her eyes peered straight into mine. 'Do you understand the seriousness of your situation?'

There was no movement in her cheekbones, no flicker of her eyelids, only a tiny shift in her chest as her breathing increased: this was no trick; my life was in her hands.

'My name is Cassie.' I got off the bed. 'What do you want me to do?'

Her shoulders relaxed as she smiled before offering her hand to me.

'It's good to meet you, Cassie. I'm Olivia.'

I took her hand and felt the touch of another person for the first time since I'd killed the president. He'd been possessed by the Archangel Michael, who was intent on unleashing a nuclear apocalypse upon the world, but it was still murder. But I didn't regret it and would do it all again if I had to. Now I wondered what I had to do to get out of this place.

My head twisted up to stare at the space where she'd just looked before I stepped close to her.

'Who do you work for, Olivia?'

She moved to the wall and knocked on it. 'Would you like a tour of the facility, Cassie?'

'Sure; what else am I going to do?' And it would be an opportunity to look for ways of escape. The door opened and I followed her outside into a lengthy, wide corridor. It didn't take long before she crushed any idea I had of getting out of there on my own.

Erasmus pointed at the ceiling. 'We're forty levels below ground, but there's an excellent ventilation system here.' The exit slid back into the wall. 'I think we have better breathable air than outside.' She strode away, and I went with her.

'What is this place?'

Her eyes brightened. 'We're a city within a city.' We'd gone fifty yards when she stopped and knocked on another empty wall. I'd been out of the cell for a minute and had already realised I wouldn't be stealing key cards or secret codes to escape. But, as the door opened, I wondered if the knock would work for me when the time came.

We stepped through the gap into what I thought was a

balcony overlooking a vast cavern. Only when she flicked a switch to turn on the lights did I witness it in all its glory: it was a scene from a science fiction film or a twisted excessive version of Spaghetti Junction. As far as I could see, bridges intertwined and sped off from where we stood; small vehicles or robotic drones moved silently along each one. Apart from Erasmus and me, there was no sign of life.

I peered over the barrier between the drop and us as a draught drifted up and brushed my hair. A crazed thought scuttled from the shadows in my head: if I jumped over the side, would my innate, not-yet-developed Arcane abilities return to save me? Or would I just splat on the stone below?

As I considered this, one of the moving vehicles approached us before stopping close to me. I wiped the suicidal jump from my mind and gazed at the box on it.

'Let me guess, Olivia: we're in the latest Amazon warehouse, and this is a job interview?'

Erasmus had a mobile phone in her hand as I spoke and she pointed it at the stationary vehicle. The side of the cart slid away to reveal a see-through rigid plastic panel; I stumbled back into the barrier when I saw its contents.

'Careful, Cassie.' She grabbed my arm to stop me from tumbling into the abyss. 'We can't have our new partnership ending before it's begun, can we?'

I shook off her grip and bent towards the box, my face close enough to see what was inside: a dark bird similar to a raven flapped its wings against its cage, but this was no raven since it had a small female head on its shoulders. She was pale, her blue eyes consumed with yearning; she opened her mouth and spoke, but no sound escaped from her prison.

A torrent of lava seethed through my veins as I turned to the doctor, the heat burning inside my skull.

'What is this, Erasmus?'

'That creature is a Gamayun. Since the end of World War II when our troops acquired it on the march to Berlin, it's been in our possession.' She checked something on her digital device as I scowled at her. 'According to the notes, the Russians used it and other supernatural creatures as spies against the Nazis.' She pointed at the cart, and the box covered its prisoner before moving from us and along the bridge. 'But I suppose you were asking more about this facility and my employers.'

I dug my nails into my fingers. 'If you want me to help you, then I have to know what's going on here.'

'All in good time, Cassie.' Erasmus moved to the wall and the door opened again. She led me back into the corridor as the silent carts continued to travel around the labyrinth we'd left. She took a right and strode fifty yards from where I assumed my cell was; then, she did the magic trick with the wall once more. I looked the other way into a vast blank space and considered making a run for it.

Erasmus turned and stared at me.

'I hope there's food in there, Olivia, because I'm starving.'

Last night's bile had disappeared, but I couldn't get the image of the bird-woman from my head. My stomach rumbled as I followed Erasmus through the latest gap in this never-ending wall.

'I'll have some food sent here.' She tapped into her device. 'You Brits like a big meaty breakfast, is that right?' Her smile showed off her brilliant white teeth. 'Or are you a vegetarian?'

My shoulders shivered as I scanned the place, my mind full of images of Alice as I stared at the rows of screens on the wall surrounding a large display in the middle. A table separated the monitors from me.

'Sausage, bacon, eggs, and toast will do.' My guts groaned at the memory of last night's food. 'But no beans. I'm allergic to beans.' Something I'd only discovered yesterday.

'Do you want anything to drink?'

'Coffee: black with plenty of sugar.' I slid into a chair.

'Your wish is my command, Cassie.' Her fingers skimmed across her device like a concert pianist's.

Then I asked her again.

'Who do you work for, Olivia, and what is this building?'

She placed the digital device on the table.

'As I said earlier, things changed quickly after you inter-vened with the president.' She pressed a button on the wood and the large screen lit up. 'Most of the cabinet who survived, those who weren't in that bunker when you arrived, were against a war with China or anyone else, especially a nuclear one. None of them will admit this publicly, but they were happy with what you did, even if you slaughtered the presi-dent and the rest of the cabinet. What your actions also did was highlight to everyone how easy it was for the supernatural to infiltrate the highest office of the United States Government.'

'I'm not sure if it's that easy. A Heavenly archangel controlled your president and the British prime minister; this was no run-of-the-mill possession.'

Shock consumed Olivia's face. 'Heaven and angels are real?'

I guessed she didn't know as much as she'd intimated, which might also apply to whoever she worked for. That could help me. I glanced at the screens and the giant board displaying an image of the damage I'd caused in that bunker.

'You don't know the half of it, Olivia. But you still haven't told me who you work for. Should I assume it's the US government?'

She regained her composure. 'It's been a week since the president's death.' It was kind of her not to say his murder at my hand or, in reality, at my mind. 'But the reaction at the highest level was swift. The vice president and the surviving cabinet members assumed control immediately. Within two hours, we had you in custody and all the proof, much to some people's disbelief, of supernatural involvement in the death and destruction in the bunker. Ironically, most of the new cabinet are deeply religious, including the former VP who is now the new president, so it didn't take much to persuade them of the gravity of the situation. And the fact a branch of the Secret Service had evidence of the supernatural going back for more than a century. After that, it was just a matter of putting an emergency policy into place.'

'You're saying the American government has always known the supernatural is real?'

'Not so much the government, but a small group of people inside the security and intelligence services.' She picked up her device and stared at the screen. 'I only discovered this six days ago, but it's the same in every country in the world. There have always been groups keeping this hidden from the public, and sometimes they've used disinformation to deflect the truth. From what I've gathered so far, that's what all the UFO and alien abduction stories have been about.'

I nearly fell from the chair. 'You're kidding? All the

UFO sightings around the world were governments spreading lies to cover up the supernatural?'

She grinned at me. 'I found it funny.'

'So, these security people with previous knowledge of the supernatural are in charge now?'

Erasmus shook her head. 'No, they're only advisors. President Dixon, the old VP who constantly clashed with his dead predecessor, felt it was time for a new broom and created a fresh security and intelligence agency to deal with the supernatural.'

The gap opened in the wall and an armed man brought a trolley in. It contained food and smelt of fried meat and scrambled eggs. They'd burnt the toast, but that was how I liked it. He pushed it between the doctor and me before leaving. I didn't wait for an invitation and helped myself, the bread crunching between my teeth as I asked her a question.

'And what do you do, Olivia, apart from interrogating innocent teenage girls?'

The aroma of coffee drifted around the room as she fumbled in her pocket. She removed a packet of cigarettes before apparently thinking better of it.

'I study quantum mechanics and EM fields.'

'What's an EM field?' I pretended to know what quantum mechanics were. If only Alice were with me, since she was the scientist in the family.

'It's an electromagnetic field.'

Bits of sausage tumbled through my throat, washed down by the sweetest coffee.

'That's fascinating, Olivia, but what's it got to do with me and the supernatural?'

She picked up her portable device and turned to the gigantic screen.

'President Dixon's new agency for the supernatural is called Section 25; it was they who hired me. After the events in the bunker, they spent the first six days creating Section 25's organisational structure and recruiting staff. Then the president took a few of his closest advisors to the small town where he grew up to complete the operational and policy details. He thought it would be away from the extended media glare consuming the nation since the death of his predecessor.'

'I guess it didn't work out too well?'

'You could say that.'

She pointed the device at the big screen, and the scene changed to one showing a massive storm of blue dust floating over a field. I put my fork down and gazed at it.

'Climate change has got that bad in the States?'

'That's not a natural storm; it's fifteen miles wide and long.'

'Blimey.' A piece of bacon got stuck between my middle teeth. 'Is that your area of expertise, Olivia? Is the blue storm caused by quantum electromagnetic fields or something?'

'Or something. Underneath it is an American town of five thousand people, and the cloud is spreading across the land; we call it the Zone.'

'Jesus, Olivia.'

'That's why you and I are here, Cassie, so you can get inside and bring President Dixon out.'

5 ALICE: THE ROAD TO NOWHERE

It was easier to hitch a ride than I expected. The woman, Julie, was on her way to Berwick and took pity on me. She even allowed me to charge my phone in the car during the journey.

'You can't be wandering these roads on your own.' She gazed at me like a disapproving parent. 'The patrols haven't reached this far yet, and you don't know who you might meet.'

I gave her my best girlish smile, fighting off the temptation to tell her sometimes it's the most innocent-looking things which are the worst. The patrols she'd mentioned were the government enforcing the State of Emergency. Prime Minister Howard, the man I'd talked down from nuclear destruction and away from the Archangel Michael's mind control, had set Britain on this path even before I'd escaped from the grounds where I'd nearly had to kill him and the others.

Britain was under attack; that's what the government and its allies in the press had told the population. And Howard had the scars to prove it, with his entourage splashing photos of his injured face all across the media. I'd stared at them many times and still couldn't remember if it was me who'd caused the cuts and bruises or if it was all a manipulation. I peered at my hands and remembered how much I'd changed in only a couple of weeks: from getting ready to start my first year at university to becoming a killer when I had to.

But it didn't matter who or what had caused the PM's scars since they had achieved the desired effect: Britain, like America, was under attack from an as-yet-unnamed enemy, and that meant special measures were implemented immediately to protect the country and the people.

And now I was passing that country by in the gloom. The road was empty, the land hissing by my window as Julie drove. And there was vampire blood on my trousers. I placed my hand over it and hoped she hadn't noticed. There was a nervous tic in her eye. I guessed it would be a two-hour drive, and I could do with getting some sleep, but the longer I left her to dwell on her thoughts, the more likely it was she'd question why a teenage girl was hitchhiking at night. Plus, there was that red stain on my leg.

'I read online the government doesn't have the resources to send too many soldiers this far north.' Internet conspiracies had become my latest fascination since I'd lost Cassie.

Julie glanced at me as she drove. 'No, that doesn't sound right. They'd already promised to recruit twenty thousand new police officers when the incident happened. Bringing in the military to patrol the country is only a temporary measure while that process is underway.' She shook her head at me. 'The government wouldn't abandon parts of Britain while we're in this State of Emergency.'

I settled into my seat, wondering what Julie would think if she knew the State of Emergency was our fault, Cassie's and mine, and all because the western world had panicked into following America after the murders of its president and his cabinet. I didn't know for sure Cassie was responsible for what had happened to President Cross and his allies, but it could only have been because of her actions.

Which meant I was the identical twin sister of the girl who'd murdered the Leader of the Free World. And I was confident it wouldn't take long before that information was splashed across the globe. As Julie drove, I glanced at my reflection in the window, trying to imagine what it was like for Cassie in America. Lucy had claimed Cassie was in a prison even she, the Devil, couldn't get into.

But the Devil lied, didn't she?

My image shimmered in the glass as a shiver ran down my spine.

'When you mention the incident, you mean the assassination?'

Julie's shoulders trembled. 'Wasn't that dreadful?'

I didn't respond. I could hardly tell her my role in it and how necessary it had been. I was fortunate in not killing the prime minister, but Cassie must have had little choice to do what she did. And I had to find her; if she was still alive.

I shook that terrible thought from my head as Julie continued. 'I think it's even worse because we never saw any of it, you know. I mean, with Kennedy, there was a sense of finality because it was filmed, but this, it's just so much worse not knowing who was behind it. And there are all the rumours flying around saying there was an attempt on the prime minister at the same time. Can you imagine how things would be now if he'd been murdered? Everything would be in chaos.' She shook her head again. 'We live in strange times.'

And they were even stranger than she realised. She was

the first human I'd conversed with since being inside Prime Minister Howard's mind, and I suddenly found her fascinating.

'Who do you think killed the president and the others?'

She puffed out her cheeks. 'It must have been terrorists. I mean, who else could it be? To get into the grounds of a secret meeting like that is unbelievable. The question is which terrorists?' Julie appeared to have a theory she was desperate to share. It was a struggle to keep my eyes open, but I asked her anyway.

'Who do you believe it was?'

'Well, think of all the security the Americans had in that place. I mean, it has to be an inside job, surely? Only last month there were all those stories of that spyware on all of our phones, recording what we do and passing the information to God knows who.' She glanced at my phone charging and shivered. 'And it was the same here with the PM. The people who attacked him must still be in the country.' She squinted over her shoulder into the back of the car as if expecting some masked terrorist to jump out at any second. 'Why else would the Americans and us be in a state of national emergency?' Julie banged one hand on the steering wheel, and the car jerked slightly. That was all I needed: this woman to get over-excited and crash. 'That's another reason why a young girl like you shouldn't be hitch-hiking on a night like this.'

I pulled my legs close to me to stay warm, but let her believe it was because I was afraid. The more she saw me as a frightened teenager, the less chance there would be she'd realise the police wanted me for murder.

'You don't think it had anything to do with what's been happening between China and Taiwan, and that American ship which was sunk in the sea separating the two countries?'

Julie shook her head. 'No, they've explained all that.' She smiled at me as if I was only a girl who didn't understand the complex grown-up world of international politics. 'It was an accident which damaged that ship, something to do with an engine failure.' She peered into the dark as she drove. 'It's a terrible shame all those sailors died, but it's all sorted now.'

She was right. When getting out of London, I'd checked the media reports regarding the repercussions of my and Cassie's actions and how they'd affected the growing tension between the West and the East. Somehow, and the rumours were that Prime Minister Howard was influential in this, the Americans and the Chinese now believed they had a common enemy which had engineered the conflict between them in the hope of starting a global war. So they'd put their animosity aside and lowered their weapons.

The ironic thing was they weren't wrong in that belief, but I wondered if they knew the common enemy was two warring archangel siblings battling for control of the planet. I also considered what the public would do if they knew the truth.

I stared at Julie in the mirror. 'There's a coup brewing.'

'What?' she said.

'People online say western democracies are under threat from internal forces, and the attacks in America and here are false flag operations.'

Julie rolled her eyes in confusion. 'What are false flags?'

'False flag operations are used to create enemies when none exist, or to deceive. The deception creates the appearance of a particular party, group, or nation being responsible for some activity, disguising the actual source of responsibility.'

Neon signs flashed by as Julie narrowed her eyes. Her gaze was still on the road as she spoke.

'You're saying you think the British and American governments carried out those attacks on themselves so they could say someone else did it, some other country? That sounds crazy.' Her cheekbones shrivelled into her face. 'They wouldn't kill their own president for that.'

My fingers scratched at the dried blood on my trousers.

'Or perhaps these regimes want to use the assaults to blame certain groups as an excuse to persecute them.'

She shook her head. 'What groups?'

How much was I prepared to tell her? Years of frustration tumbled out of me before I could stop the words from taking shape.

'The same people some are constantly pushing back against: the disenfranchised, the rebellious voices, minorities, the oppressed, those that are different, and the left behind.'

There was doubt in her face as she stared at me. 'I think maybe you're tired and I'm keeping you awake. Why don't you rest, and I'll wake you when we get to the Holy Island?'

'Okay.' I didn't need a second invitation, turning my head from her and closing my eyes. It was a fitful journey as I drifted in and out of restless sleep. I filled my dreams with what had happened to Cassie and our mother and how Lucy had betrayed us. Occasionally, I'd flicker awake and peer into the darkness outside.

The digital clock in the car's dashboard said it was 3am when Julie pulled over.

'Are you sure this is where you want to be? The sea

covers the causeway until the morning. What will you do while you wait?'

I brushed the sleep from my face. 'I checked online: it's safe to cross in an hour until mid-day.'

I hoped eight hours would be plenty of time to get into the Nexus, find Bella, question her, and then out and off the island again. If that weren't enough, the causeway would reopen from five until just after midnight. If I hadn't got what I wanted by then, I assumed I'd be in deep trouble.

Julie seemed concerned about leaving a teenage girl on a dark road in the early hours of the morning. 'Are you sure you'll be okay?'

'I'm sure,' I said as I got out of the car. 'Thanks again for the lift.'

She drove off and I checked where I was. There were signs to Lindisfarne at the side of the road, including warnings about the tide. The causeway would open in an hour. I could get a lift to the island, but I didn't expect much traffic at four o'clock in the morning. Public transport would run buses from nine, but I couldn't wait that long.

I pulled the zip up to the top of my jacket, hoping it would keep the chill out. I knew where I wanted to be on the island, where Bella was imprisoned, and was impatient to get there.

The car disappeared in the distance as I headed towards the Nexus.

I spat egg over the floor before I choked on it.

'What? What did you say?'

'The cloud is supernatural and covers the whole town of Valhalla, Maryland.' She pressed on the device in her hand, and the screen changed to a clip of the blue substance appearing above the town and spreading everywhere. 'This was taken from a government satellite and shows how quickly the haze covered every part of Valhalla. Then we have these clips uploaded online before it went silent.'

She played several short videos from inside the town as the blue mist descended and spread. In seconds, it enclosed a water tower as cars disappeared beneath a sapphire wave, moving into it but never reappearing. Next, it crept into buildings and consumed them as the azure flowed through streets and over everything in its way. And then there were the people. Initially, a few residents laughed at the cloud as it approached; maybe they thought it was part of some trick, but when the first group vanished and didn't come out, those close by ran and screamed, disappearing off-camera. I watched a dozen clips, and a chill overtook my heart as the screen froze on an ocean blue shimmer.

'It's not a natural event?'

'That was the initial thought: that perhaps it was something ecological or related to climate change, but then it consumed everything in its path and the government started evacuating places. And we sent the military inside in full protective breathing gear.' She took a deep breath. 'This is the surveillance footage broadcast to base.'

The video was from headcams, shaky and unfocused. The soldiers' voices were low and cautious. Their cameras pointed through the cloud, but only found more of the blue. The large screen was divided into eight smaller parts, with a name in the bottom corner of each. They transmitted images of thick mist before every one of them cut out after thirty-seven seconds exactly.

'What happened to them?' I'd lost my appetite and pushed the plate from me.

'We don't know. We would have sent drones in first, but because President Dixon is inside, the decision was taken to send troops in before that. That America would lose two presidents in less than a week was unthinkable for many.'

'So you sent the machines in next?'

'A hundred drones went in, from every direction possible, but we received nothing from them from the start.'

The stress of it must have got to her and she lit a cigarette. I moved back a little, though I knew it wouldn't make much difference.

'Aren't the public freaking out?'

'The cover story is of a serious chemical leak, so that's keeping the majority away. The National Guard stationed around the cloud deals with any who are too curious.

Including you and I, only a dozen people know President Dixon is trapped inside.'

'What makes you believe the mist is supernatural?'

'What else could it be?'

'Maybe one of America's enemies created it, or it's a terrorist attack.'

Erasmus shook her head. 'No, there's nothing natural about it. Which is why Section 25 sent me to talk to you.' She took a long drag on the cigarette. 'We need your help.'

'To do what?'

'Get inside, find Dixon and stop this thing from devouring the whole of America.' She blew smoke into the air. 'You killed the last president, so you owe us to save this one.'

I didn't hesitate. 'I appreciate the offer, Olivia, but I have to refuse. From what you've shown me, if I step in there, I'm never coming back out.'

She stubbed the ciggy on the table, the end of it smouldering into the wood.

'If you don't help us, you're never getting out of this building, anyway.' There was a fire in her eyes and ice in her voice.

'You can't threaten me, Doctor. I danced with the Devil and survived.' I twisted my head to look around the room. 'Your little boys-playing-with-toys organisation doesn't scare me.'

Erasmus rolled the dead cancer stick across the table.

'What if I said we'd release you from here and reunite you with your sister?'

I stumbled, my body inching out of the chair until I steadied myself by grabbing the table.

'What?'

'I can have a contract in front of you within minutes,

guaranteeing your freedom and knowledge of the where-abouts of your twin, Alice.'

'You've known all along who I am?'

Her smile annoyed me. 'I thought it best to see how truthful you would be with me.'

The smouldering cigarette irritated my nose and throat, while her continued grin was eminently punchable.

'Where is Alice?' A nervous spasm travelled through my legs and up my body. I scratched at my palm until the blood came.

'Your sister is alive, Cassie, and still in England. That's all I can say for now. However, if you agree to what I ask, then Section 25 will honour our promise to you.'

'You'll let me go and tell me where Alice is?'

'I guarantee it.'

I forced my spine into the chair, studying her face and considering what options I had. I'd been prepared to return to my cell for however long it took for me to escape. My Arcane abilities may have vanished, but I was convinced they'd reappear at some point. Then there would be no stopping me. But now, with this news about my sister, I couldn't hang around.

'Is Alice well? Is she like me and imprisoned?'

'You mean did the British authorities lock her up after she murdered your prime minister?'

It was another blow to my heart. 'Did she do that?' And how did Erasmus know these things?

'No, I'm sorry, Cassie; that last part wasn't true. Your sister stopped the PM from pushing the nuclear option, killing no one, and she's roaming free now. I guess her mission must have differed from yours.'

The blood continued to drip from my palm.

'How do you know all this?'

She worked the controls on the big screen again, changing it from video to a selection of photographs. I recognised where they had been taken immediately: half a dozen were from the battlefield outside the mansion where the previous president had been in a bunker ready to start the end of the world. The images were of bodies on the ground, supernatural creatures that had fought on both sides. The other photos were from inside the building, of security guards ripped apart.

'There were a few survivors from these, and they've been our guests deep in this building, like you have. It didn't take long for them to tell us about two supernatural gangs at war with each other; most of them provided both you and your sister's names. Only one of these creatures refused to talk. I think she's a friend of yours.'

Erasmus changed the screen again to show a large photograph of a teenage girl: Claudia.

'She's here?' Thank God she was alive. Without Claudia's help, I wouldn't have got inside that mansion, and it was her tactics that had left me clear to finish the president. So I owed her a lot.

I owed her my life.

'The girl who isn't a girl isn't doing too well, I'm afraid.' Erasmus moved closer to me. 'Understand, Cassie, I'm only a functionary here; those in charge don't have my patience. This issue with President Dixon and whatever that blue cloud is, coming after an attack on the United States, has left many frazzled. If there isn't a resolution soon, then your friend and others will suffer.'

I stood and pushed away from Erasmus. 'Take me to her.'

We exited the room and went down the corridor. There was nothing but white space everywhere, no sign there was life in the building beyond us, yet I knew that was untrue. I thought of the Gamayun again, trapped inside that tiny moving cage; how many other supernatural creatures were imprisoned here? And why was I concerned about them? I'd spent over two years travelling across the north of England, killing monsters, and now the only thoughts I had were of protecting such things.

Erasmus continued to walk ahead, making no attempt at conversation, and I was happy with that. I thought about how my life had transformed since I'd met Alice. Being with her and what we'd discovered had changed my attitude to the supernatural world: our time together convinced me not everything non-human was a monster. It wasn't only our encounters with peaceful creatures like Kai the Warwitch and the unfortunates in Limbo and Purgatory, but how Medusa the Gorgon and Scooby the Hellhound had helped in the search for our mother. Then there was Vika Vistala, the Baobhan Sith, a Scottish vampire who'd given us Scooby so we could get into Hell.

And then there was Claudia, another vamp who'd aided me. Erasmus called her my friend, but I hardly knew her, had spent only a few hours with her. But she'd let me read her mind and, in doing so, had created an unexpected bond between us. It also allowed me to see some of the terrible things Claudia had suffered in the two hundred years of her human and vampire existence. There was a kindness to her, to this vampire; something I'd never have believed possible a few weeks ago when I was determined to kill everything I saw as a monster.

Erasmus stopped before me and did her thing with the wall again. There had to be some infrared system she accessed to identify all the invisible doors. She smiled those flawless white teeth at me as the gap opened. I thought how the worst monsters you'd meet are the ones who appear perfect on the outside.

She stepped to the side as I peered through the door. The cell was half the size of mine, with no bathroom or sink and only a bucket near the bed. Claudia was chained to the wall with manacles around her feet, hands and neck. Blood stained her clothes, her face crisscrossed with fresh scars. I barged past Erasmus and threw myself at Claudia, her body trembling against me as we hugged in the silence.

Claudia shook her head as we let go. 'I'd hoped you'd escaped.'

'There's still time for that.' I made sure Erasmus and whoever was watching heard that. 'How are you?'

When she smiled, it looked as if one of her front teeth was cracked. 'I've stayed in better places.' She gazed over my shoulder at Erasmus. 'And I've been in worse.'

I gripped her hands and turned to the doctor.

'You have to get her clean and out of here. Then we can speak about rescuing your president.'

I didn't care about him or any of them. I'd get Claudia away and we'd both look for Alice, and we wouldn't need any help from Erasmus or these Section 25 goons to do it.

Erasmus shook her head. 'That's not my call, Cassie. I received special dispensation to talk to you, and that's it.'

'And you shouldn't even have got that.'

A large shadow followed that booming voice, and I wondered how much more trouble I was in.

7 ALICE: THE TIDE IS HIGH

Something small ran across my foot and into the grass as I decided to try my teleportation abilities again. Before the altercation with Marv and his vamps, and since stopping the prime minister from setting off a nuclear war, I'd teleported once by accident. I'd hidden away on the back of a truck driving north from London, but on its stop outside Leeds, I'd slipped out to get some food. Unfortunately, as I was about to spend the last of my cash on a cheese sandwich, the girl behind the counter must have recognised me from the news.

Her screams and wildly pointing finger not only shocked everyone in the motorway services, but alerted the two coppers drinking coffee nearby. Luckily, there were no armed soldiers around, but the police officers reacted more quickly than I'd expected.

The woman had hold of me before I could move from the counter, with her colleague not far behind her. Thankfully, she wasn't too strong for me, so it was easy to shake her off and sprint outside, the plastic wrapper of the packet of sandwiches rippling out of my pocket.

I knew I was quick and fancied my chances of getting away from them. All I had to do was get across the motorway and into the trees on the other side. There was a barrier just ahead and, as the policeman shouted at me to stop, I lifted one foot to jump.

That's when the Taser hit me in the arm.

My legs gave way as a surge of electricity pulsed through me. A jackhammer pounded every muscle and bone, and I bit into my lip in shock. The air smelt of burning rubber and my mouth tasted of copper as I went numb. I fell to the pavement and rolled to my side. A drizzle of rain dropped on my face as the two officers raced towards me.

The jolt must have triggered something inside me. The next thing I knew, I was throwing up in the grass somewhere near Newcastle. I lay there in the dark for an age before the control of my body returned to me.

I only realised where I was because of the road signs, staring at them as I wiped the vomit from my mouth. It tasted horrible, but it didn't stop me from eating the sarnie once I'd cleared my face. The teleportation didn't work again when I tried it later, not until I was submerged below the gang of vampires in that house in Gateshead.

So that's how I'd ended up hitching a lift to Lindisfarne.

Now, as I was across the causeway and so close to my destination, I tried again.

I closed my eyes, focused on that room I'd visited before, and visualised the coffin attached to the wall containing Bella's body. Inside my mind, I saw the creatures imprisoned in that building, remembered the people who'd betrayed Cassie and me, and heard the voice of the vampire who might be Dracula's sister. Her words echoed inside my skull as I reached towards her in my mind. I grasped for her prison attached to the wall, but it wouldn't work, no matter how hard I tried.

I gave up in frustration and walked over the road towards the Lindisfarne Inn. There was time to kill before the water receded and I could walk to the Holy Island via the Pilgrim's Way. The island's official website mentioned the journey as about sixty minutes across sand and mud. I didn't have the Wellington boots it recommended, but it didn't matter. I just had to get there. And I could always go barefoot.

For protection from the cold, I crept to the back of the pub, found a doorway in the corner and curled up there. A heady aroma of alcohol and seawater drifted over me. I removed my phone and checked my messages, still hoping Cassie would somehow get in touch. I refused to believe she was dead, sensing in my bones I would have known.

There were no texts from her, but I spent the time scrolling through the ones from Medusa. My friend the Gorgon had adjusted to her new life better than I'd expected, but all her concerns were for Cassie and me. I pushed into the concrete, my face half inside the shadows, peering at the sky. The hour dragged by, a combination of the chilled air and my burning guilt forming a constant irritation through every part of me.

The internet was no comfort since it was full of terrible stories of armed police and troops in Britain and America acting as the political will of their respective leaders. The new leadership in the US had clamped down on everything immediately after what they called the assassination, but what I knew to be Cassie liberating the world from nuclear Armageddon. The fact she'd had to kill America's leaders to do it was regrettable but necessary. I'd been lucky in talking the prime minister out of Michael's influence.

But maybe the two of us had only delayed the inevitable; there was still plenty of media talk of those events starting World War III. Now Britain's State of Emergency, while not as severe as the American one, had the whole country on edge. Yet here I was waiting to break into a secret government organisation that collected supernatural creatures. Only they weren't collecting, but imprisoning them; perhaps even experimenting on them for all I knew. As the hour ticked away, I considered the fate of those I'd left behind the last time I was there.

A brilliant sunrise greeted me as I exited the pub's grounds and headed for the start of the Pilgrim's Way. The sea had parted to reveal the path. A line of posts marked the route over the mudflats. It started a short distance along the causeway close to a shed on stilts, built there for the salvation of motorists who gambled with fate and lost. From this refuge, they could gaze over the incoming tide and reflect on their misfortune while their car disappeared beneath the waves. I hoped it wasn't an omen for my mission on the island.

The sun wiped away most of the gloom as I surveyed my destination. I removed my socks and shoes and planted my feet into the sludge. The surface was cold and wet, but at least I'd have clean and dry footwear when I reached the other side. I plodded towards the first posts lining the path, and my toes disappeared into the gloop.

The mud stretched into the horizon, but I didn't let it deter me. As I trudged along, my thoughts turned to what I'd do at the Nexus. The last time I was there, with Cassie, the leader of the organisation, Dr Rivers, tried to imprison both of us. We only just escaped with our lives, and that was when we were fighting for each other. So how could I sneak in, find what I wanted, and get out safely on my own?

This thought consumed me as the wind bit at my cheeks and the bouquet of the departing sea wafted up to my nose. A taste of saltwater settled on the end of my tongue every time I opened my mouth to take a breath.

After a few hundred metres, I reached a pilgrim's shelter perched on stilts above the endless mudflats. A flock of seagulls circled above me as if expecting their next meal. Perhaps the constant squawks were their way of telling me to turn back. I ignored them and slogged on. Whatever barriers I encountered inside the Nexus, I'd have to deal with them.

I plodded onwards through soft brown mud and tidal streams rippling around my ankles. The marker posts passed by me one by one, but still, their endless line stretched to the vanishing point. Occasionally, I'd come across bits of firm ground covered in thin layers of grass, which stank so badly I had to cover my nose at the same time as dodging the gaps in the dark sludge.

The reeking black mire was behind me as I entered the last mile of firmer brown muck sprinkled with tiny shells nipping at my toes. The wind buffeted the back of my head and screamed in my ears. Birds hovered and squealed around me, a flapping guard of feathered onlookers guiding me to my destination.

Across the mudflats, an enormous noise erupted over the howl of nature: a vast colony of seals barked as I made my barefoot approach to Lindisfarne. The morning had broken as I stared at the grime caking my ankles and toes. I hadn't brought anything to clean them. Reluctant to cover my dirty feet, I sloped into the car park in search of something to remove the mud. After a fruitless five minutes, I scraped them over the grass and the ground cut into my skin. It was the best I could do before putting my socks and shoes back on, watching as a dribble of blood dripped from my foot.

The island appeared deserted, but I knew it wasn't, even though it was too early for tourists. I strode past the priory and the ruins, aiming for the sea ahead of me. I marched towards the lookout tower and beyond the war memorials. The harbour was on one side, an expanse of space on the other. That's where I needed to be.

I picked up speed and jogged across the dry earth, hoping the underground entrance was still there, that it hadn't been removed after Cassie and I had escaped. Then, I saw the smoke lifting from the ground and knew it led into the tunnels. I ran to it and knelt at the metal opening. It took me a minute to drag the cover off, and dirt covered my fingers by the end. I wiped them on the grass and climbed down to reach the intersection below the island. When I got there, there were three directions to choose from. I picked the right one and headed to the Nexus.

The tunnel was damp, narrow and stank of the sewers. Rats scurried along the sides while clumps of spiders hung from the walls. I strode past them and towards the lift at the end. It looked no different from when I was there last. The blade and the stakes were in my jacket as I pressed the button and entered the lift. I sent it to the first floor, removing the knife as I headed up.

All I had to do now was fight my way through an organisation that wanted to imprison me.

8 CASSIE: CLAUDIA

The shadow turned into a towering bloke wearing a combat uniform with the name Commander Bolt stitched into it. He had a face of granite, brown eyes so dark you couldn't see any light in them, and a mop of candy floss hair plastered to his head. Even without saying another word, he had the air of a man who slept in that uniform and kept a Confederate flag in his living room.

'The prisoners are not allowed out of their cells, Doctor Erasmus.' His voice was like a scythe cutting through me. 'This isn't what we agreed on.'

But Erasmus was unfazed by it or him. 'Do you want to get the president back and save Valhalla, Commander?' She glanced at me. 'Because she's the only one who can do that.'

He stepped closer to her, his shadow looming over Claudia and me.

'I've got a squad of elite troops ready to enter that blue cloud at any minute, Doctor.' His head peered over the top of hers so they looked like a strange amalgamation of body parts. 'That's far better than trusting some sixteen-year-old girl who's already assassinated one president of the United States.'

Erasmus pushed up to his impressive chest, defiance dripping from her every word.

'If you're desperate to send your people to their deaths, again, be my guest, Commander Bolt; you can then answer to the higher-ups at your leisure.'

He ignored us and sneered at her. 'The desperation isn't mine, Doctor.' His gaze bored into her, his expression that of a man who'd seen the worst the world had to offer and it hadn't fazed him. 'A bunch of scientists believing in the supernatural is a bit rich, don't you think?'

'The truth of that is already here, Commander. You've seen the same evidence I have.' She turned from him to me. 'You've examined the exhibits we have in this facility, and I know you've scoured the videos of President Cross's death several times. If none of these things makes you believe in the supernatural, I'm not sure what will.'

I had no interest in their pissing contest.

'I'll save your president and the town, but I need to get my friend cleaned up first.'

While they went outside and considered that request, I leant into Claudia and pushed my palm up to her mouth. I pretended to take no notice of Bolt and Erasmus, who were whispering to each other in the corridor. Then the Commander stormed off and Olivia touched my shoulder.

'It's all been arranged. I'll get you somewhere nicer than this and we can formulate a plan. We need you inside the Zone within twelve hours.'

That seemed hasty. 'Why so soon?'

'Because the Zone is moving again. At its present rate, it will consume the next town in fourteen hours.'

'Hasn't it been evacuated?' What had these idiots been doing, wasting all this time on me?

Dark shadows crept along Olivia's face. 'They didn't want to panic anyone.' She rubbed at her throat. 'The top brass thought the situation would be over by now and...'

'And some of them are like Bolt. They think the cloud is science that's gone wrong or an attack which can be easily explained and dealt with.'

'Something like that, yes.'

'How many people are in that town?'

'Its population is twenty thousand.'

Shit! Was I prepared to have that on my conscience if I could prevent it? Of course I wasn't. Not that I knew how I could stop a deadly supernatural blue cloud travelling across the US.

'Okay, I'll go, but I need another condition before I do; something as well as the guarantee of my freedom and you helping me find Alice.'

'What condition is that?'

'Let Claudia leave.'

Erasmus didn't hesitate. 'Agreed.'

The doctor pressed something on her phone, and Claudia's manacles separated from her body. The one around her throat came away from the wall, but stayed attached to her flesh. I pointed at it as I lifted her from the bed.

'And remove that.'

'Only a technician can do that.'

'Why?' Erasmus hesitated this time. 'And don't lie to me.'

Claudia answered for her. 'There's an explosive device in my neck.' She glared at Erasmus. 'They take no chances here.'

I pulled Claudia with me and out of the cell as Erasmus stepped back into the corridor. I scowled at her.

'Remove the manacle and the bomb, Olivia.'

She held up her hands. 'That's out of my control, Cassie, and we're running out of time. We need to get you ready and your team prepped to leave.' As she spoke, a noiseless cart drifted towards us. It was bigger than the one I'd seen earlier, large enough to transport three people across this vast underground landscape.

'What do you mean, a team? I'm not going inside that cloud with any of your soldiers.' I continued to make conditions I was sure I couldn't keep.

'We'll talk about that after you've freshened up.' She didn't elaborate any further as we climbed into the cart and she gave it instructions. We travelled down another endless white corridor before descending to the junction of bridges I'd witnessed earlier. 'Put your seat belts on.'

We did as instructed before dropping a dozen feet to the bridge below us. It was like being at the funfair as we descended, and the rapid drop created a wind that blew our hair into our faces. When I'd pushed mine away and the cart was horizontal once more, we sped along the underground road for at least two minutes. I held Claudia as she closed her eyes, and I assumed it was from tiredness and not fear of our journey. I pressed my free hand to her lips again so she could taste my blood dripping there: the sooner she regained her full strength, the better.

The first time I did it, back in her cell, I hadn't considered if it would be dangerous for her to drink my Arcane blood. An angel and a demon once tried to consume Alice and my souls, but whatever we have inside us isn't like a human soul, and it poisoned both of them. I'd gambled that drinking my blood wouldn't do the same to Claudia, and it appeared as if I was right. She rested on me as we continued our journey into the depths of the abyss.

I engaged Erasmus in conversation as we went.

'What do you call this place?'

A rainbow of lights flickered around us as smaller carts transported their unknown cargo throughout the building. The doctor gazed at me as we moved over one bridge, and then another.

'Have you heard of Area 51?'

Even with the seatbelt on, I used my free hand to grip the side of the cart.

'Is that where we are?'

She shot me a mischievous smile as we travelled through a dark part of the underground, the gloom only highlighting the whiteness of her teeth.

'It might be.' She laughed and it echoed around our cavernous surroundings, bouncing off the walls and unnerving me.

I pulled Claudia closer to me in the half-light, but she appeared to be asleep.

'I thought it would be colder this far underground.'

'This place is a marvel of modern engineering. The heating system is only one of its many wonders.'

'Are there aliens and UFOs in here?'

She laughed again. 'Not that I'm aware of.'

'What's your relationship with Commander Bolt?'

Erasmus narrowed her eyes. 'Pardon?'

It was my turn to laugh. 'I don't mean like that. Is he in charge of you? Is he your boss?'

She pushed a stray hair from her eye.

'Well, thank goodness. I wondered what was going through your mind when you said that.'

Claudia continued to slumber in my arms. It was a

curious sensation since she was smaller than me, and I felt like I was her mother for a brief second.

'Does he run Section 25?'

'Dear God, no.' She shook her head. 'That doesn't bear thinking about. Bolt is in charge of the military wing, but he answers to the higher-ups just as I do. I was seconded to the science division a week ago.' She twisted her gaze at the vastness and lights around us. 'Most of this is as new to me as it is to you.'

'If Section 25 is an organisation dealing with the supernatural, why bring in a scientist?'

'I asked them the same question.' She appeared to be warming to the conversation as we sped through the maze of bridges. To stop me from getting dizzy, I focused on her face and not what was passing by us in a rush; we were on the rollercoaster to end all rollercoasters. 'Again, I'm fairly new to all this, and even with a few doubters like Bolt, there is a consensus the supernatural is only undiscovered science.'

'Magic's just science we don't understand yet?'

'Yes; Arthur C Clarke. Have you read his work?'

I shook my head and Claudia murmured a little. 'My sister said it to me once.'

'Well, Clarke also said, and I'm quoting, "Any sufficiently advanced technology is indistinguishable from magic." I think most of Section 25's scientists, if not all of them, but the biologists and anthropologists, believe supernatural creatures are an offshoot of humanity we don't fully understand yet. Therefore there is a movement to gather, study, and analyse the supernatural.' She stared into the space surrounding us. 'And that's why part of this place has been hastily developed since your encounter with the previous president.'

'I'm guessing Commander Bolt doesn't share this view?'

'In my experience, the military and science rarely get on, unless we're creating weapons for them or getting their grunts to kill quicker and better.' She didn't hide the disappointment in her voice.

'How many supernatural beings have you imprisoned here?'

She sighed heavily. 'I'm unsure, Cassie.' She looked me straight in the eye. 'I don't know everything that goes on here, but yes, some of it is unethical and unnecessary.' She put her hand on my arm. 'This is the beginning of a new chapter of history, and mistakes will happen, but I'm convinced that, once President Dixon returns and we neutralise the Zone, things will change for the better. Then it won't be so brutal in parts.' She squeezed my arm. 'But we need your help.'

'No pressure then.'

The cart jolted to a halt and Claudia jerked awake.

'What, where am I?'

I gripped her hand. 'It's okay; we're going to get refreshed.'

We climbed out and followed Erasmus into another empty corridor; it must have cost a fortune in white paint to decorate the place. I helped Claudia as Erasmus took us into a vast room. This was no cell, resembling an expensive hotel suite, with two large beds, an en suite bathroom, three sofas, a big-screen TV, and plush carpets. There was even a trolley full of fresh food.

'Eat, drink, shower and freshen up, girls. I'll be back in an hour to discuss who'll be on your team for the incursion into the Zone.'

There she was, talking about a team again. I ignored it and went to the trolley. There was plenty for me, but not what Claudia needed to regain her strength. I grabbed Olivia before she left.

'Claudia needs a different sustenance.'

'I'm well aware of that, Cassie; look under the trolley.'

Then she left without another word. The door slid into the wall like all the other times, and I couldn't see any obvious way out. I went to the trolley, pulled back the covering and retrieved the plastic bags from underneath: there were six of them filled with blood. I gave one to Claudia.

'We've got to get your strength up before you leave here.'

She ripped it open with her teeth and devoured it in a gulp. When she'd finished, she wiped spots of red from her face.

'The only place I'm going is with you, Cassie.'

I handed her another bag. 'What do you mean?'

'Isn't it obvious?' She gulped down the blood. 'I'm heading into the Zone with you.'

9 ALICE: NEXUS

I stepped out of the lift ready for a confrontation, only to find emptiness. Not too long ago, it was a library overflowing with books and ancient documents. Now, all I had for company was the dust and the cobwebs; even the piano was gone. I strode towards the end of the room and the gap where Bella's coffin had been.

The wall was cold as I ran my fingers over the space. I couldn't let this turn of events dampen my determination to find Bella: without her, there was no Dracula, and minus him, I had no chance of finding my mother. And I didn't know how I'd get to Cassie without my mother's help. It meant I'd have to search the rest of the Nexus.

Then the voice stopped me.

'You and your sister ruined everything.'

I turned to face the woman who'd wanted to experiment on me. Perhaps she still did.

'What's happened here, Dr Rivers?' My focus was on her while I checked there was no danger.

She moved towards me in silence, her wheelchair gliding across the dusty floor.

'Don't worry, Alice, I won't attack you.' She smiled, but I didn't believe her.

'You did when I was here before, with those metal limbs of yours.' Sitting there, she appeared so unassuming, but I knew better. Beneath the blanket covering her legs were metallic weapons of mass destruction, which Cassie and I had only just escaped from last time.

Her smile disappeared, replaced with a face full of regret. 'They removed my prosthetics like they took the Nexus from me.' She whipped the cover off to reveal a space where her legs had been. 'It's your fault, but I don't hold any grudges against you or your sister.'

A breeze came from somewhere and ruffled my hair. Had I thought the lift was the only entrance? I scanned the room to see where she'd come in, preparing for an attack.

'There's always more than one way in and out of everywhere, Alice.'

My fingers dug into my palm. 'What happened here?'

She pressed something on the arm of her wheelchair and moved towards me. My nails bit harder into my skin.

'You and Cassandra happened here.' She stopped five feet from me. 'Though I blame myself for everything. If I'd treated you differently, the world might be a different place now.'

'I'm losing patience with you, Rivers.'

'Your actions, yours and Cassandra's, in London and America changed the whole shebang. Not only at the Nexus, but across the planet. What comes next is on your heads, yours and your sister's.'

'We saved the world.'

Rivers shook her head, staring at me as if I was a child. 'No, Alice, all that talk of a nuclear war was a smokescreen.

Governments do this from time to time to increase the control they have over the public.'

'You're wrong, Doctor. I was there with the prime minister. I was inside his mind fighting the influence of the Archangel Michael. Cassie did the same in the US with the president.'

'And she killed him and all his cabinet. And you say this was because of a creature, a Biblical archangel, which the Nexus hasn't come across in over five hundred years.' She shook her head again. 'I've lived with the supernatural all my life, but angels and demons, God and the Devil, don't exist. What you encountered must have been something else, shapeshifters probably, but it doesn't matter. The consequences of your actions are real.'

Rivers looked a lot older than she was, her eyes shrinking into the weathered parchment of her face.

'The government took the Nexus from you?'

'After the assassination of the president, the American and British authorities came to a secret agreement regarding where the biggest terrorist threat to them was.'

'The supernatural?'

The doctor nodded. 'Other world governments soon followed. For centuries, it was left to groups like the Nexus to collect and deal with the supernatural, keeping our activities away from ordinary folk. Now, thanks to you and your sister, the supernatural will be weaponised or wiped out. It's only a matter of time before some nation reveals the truth to the public. We're in a supernatural arms race now, and there's no place for people like me or organisations such as the Nexus.'

I scanned the emptiness of the room once more. 'The government shut you down and removed all your prisoners.'

'You mean our exhibits.' She peered at me with narrow

eyes. 'But they didn't take everything, not yet. They don't have what you came for.'

My heart skipped a beat and I struggled to breathe. 'Is Bella here?'

Dr Ellen Rivers wheeled closer to me. 'Five hundred years of haphazard record-keeping means this new organisation the government created to oversee supernatural activity, AEGIS, isn't quite on top of removing all the exhibits from this island. But it won't take them long. I'll tell you where Bella is if you promise me something.'

The blood pumped in my veins and inside my forehead. Could I believe her, or was this another of her manipulations? How could she know what Cassie and I had done, but not realise how close the world had come to nuclear Armageddon?

'What do you want?'

Rivers turned from me and towards the far wall. I followed without an invitation. She didn't face me as she spoke.

'Behind here is what you seek. The vampire is yours if you do as I ask.'

People always want to make bargains with me. I put my hands on the arms of her chair, wheeled her around, and peered at her.

'I'm a fugitive in Britain. The police are searching for me for at least one murder. I've lost my sister and mother and have no friends. I have nowhere to stay and no transportation. I have no money. The only clothes I have are the ones I'm wearing. I haven't had a shower in over a week. Vampire blood is under my nails and on my trousers. What can I give you?'

She reached into her pocket and I put my hand on her arm.

'I have no weapons anymore, Alice, only a gift for you.' Weariness seeped out of her.

I let go. 'One wrong move, Doctor.'

Rivers removed a piece of paper and handed it to me.

'You remember the code we found on Bella in 1940?'

'Of course, I do.' I'd deciphered a small part of it. 'Why are you giving this to me?'

'So you can hand it back to Bella when you free her from the coffin.'

'And what do you get?'

'I want you to take me with you, Alice. There's nothing for me here now. With my knowledge, I'd be useful in helping you find Cassandra and your mother.'

It was a ridiculous idea, but I didn't tell her. 'Show me the vampire.'

Rivers pressed another button on her wheelchair and the wall parted like the Red Sea. Bella's suited skeleton hung from the inside. The only thing preventing her bones from tumbling to the floor was the stake punched through her heart.

'You can release her, Alice, but there's no guarantee what she'll do.'

My hand was on the wood, a chill running from it and through my skin. I needed to make a deal with this vamp, but I had nothing to bargain with. I gripped the stake and placed my other arm around Bella's bony shoulder. I dragged the suit of bones close to me as I pulled the wood far enough out so Bella wasn't pinned to the wall.

The dead vampire came away from the concrete as I kept the stake pressed into the spot where her heart should have been. I took her in my arms and moved from the wall. I expected dust and an aroma of death, but all I got was the smell of lemons. Bella's skull peered into my eyes as I went into the middle of the room. Her bones were nothing to carry, as light as paper in my grasp, but there were centuries of tales on this parchment I was about to unfold.

Rivers stared at me through flabbergasted eyes. 'What are you doing?'

I ignored her question and stepped towards a large table. I laid Bella's suit of bones on the top, ensuring the stake stayed in place. Then I removed the blade from my jacket.

'There's no point bringing her back to life without leverage.' I placed the knife next to where her throat should reappear and put my other hand on the wood. 'And now I have it.' I pulled the weapon out of her chest in one go.

Rivers moved from us and towards the lift, unable to hide the terror on her face.

'Good luck with that.'

Blood, muscle, and ligament sprang from nothing and over Bella's skeleton. I concentrated on her face, focused on her empty eyes as milky pupils popped into life. Her mouth and lips appeared, already formed into a smile. Her cheeks blew up like inflatable balloons, with a long white mane flowering on her head and flowing down her shoulders.

'We must stop meeting like this, Alice. People will talk.' Her voice jolted a little because of the blade pressed against her resurrected throat.

I stared straight at her. 'You've dyed your hair.'

Bella flashed her eyes at me. 'What can I say? I did it for a boy. Are you going to let me up? This table isn't that comfortable.'

'We have to make a deal first.'

A gargled laugh escaped from Bella's mouth. 'I'm guessing a lot's changed since I saw you last.'

'You don't know the half of it.'

'Where's your twin?'

'I'll tell you later. I need to ask you a question.'

'Only one?'

'It'll do for now.'

'I'm all ears.'

'Are you Dracula's sister?'

'What?' Rivers had a coughing fit behind me.

Bella grinned and pushed her flesh into the blade at her throat. A trickle of blood slithered down it.

'I suppose people had to find out, eventually.'

'Is your real name Isabella?'

'Ironic, isn't it?'

The tyres on Rivers's wheelchair squealed as she rolled next to me. But it wasn't me she was interested in.

'You mean to say, after all this time, your name really is Bella, and Dracula is your brother?'

Bella continued to grin. 'What can I say? I'm an enigma wrapped inside a puzzle hidden inside a riddle. If you'd been kind to me all these years, Ellen, I would have told you everything.'

Dr Rivers looked as if she was about to explode, her face as red as an apple, her eyes wider than the horizon. She grabbed my hand and pushed the blade into Bella's throat. I had to move back to get her off.

And then it was too late.

Bella was off the table and across the other side of the room before I could shake Rivers from the knife.

Rivers glared at me. 'Now you've got us both killed.'

'What is it you want with my little brother, Alice?'

I stepped back and put the table between Bella and me; Rivers could fend for herself.

'He's abducted my mother.'

Bella laughed and shook her head. 'The last of the

Nephilim? He always was a lovesick puppy, but I didn't realise how desperate he must have become. I blame our parents for that. They were far too soft on him. Me, on the other hand...'

'I need your help to find them.'

Bella ran her fingers through her hair. 'And why would I do that?'

I glared at Rivers. 'Because I saved you from her. I came here to rescue you from the Nexus, and I have.'

Her movement was a blur, quicker than any vampire I'd encountered, nearly as fast as an archangel. Her hand was on Rivers's throat before I'd stopped talking.

'Something has happened here since I spoke to you last. Tell me everything.'

So I gave her a short version, starting with travelling through time to see our mother in the hospital, our battles with Michael and Lucy's betrayal, the Nephilim and the Arcane, and finishing with my struggle with the possessed British Prime Minister and Cassie's assassination of the President of the United States.

'And now the government has put Rivers out to pasture and closed down the Nexus. They'll be here for you soon.' I didn't know if that was true or not, but I had to make her believe it.

When the lights went out and the bullets started flying, I knew something was wrong.

10 CASSIE: THE BOMB

Claudia dripped blood to the floor as I stared at her. 'Why would you come with me into the blue cloud of death? Don't you want to get away from here?'

She finished her second bag of red liquid.

'I do, but only with you.' She wiped her face with her free hand. 'You can't go into the Zone on your own, and Erasmus has already said she's putting a team together, so I have to be on it. Who else will keep your back covered?'

'Me, you and a bunch of soldiers inside the supernatural cloud; yeah, I can see that going well.'

Claudia got another bag and I suddenly lost my appetite.

'Sure, they'll send a few grunts along to monitor us, but that's not the team she's talking about.'

'What do you mean?'

'Think about it, Cassie; who would you want with you to deal with a seemingly unstoppable supernatural force?'

'More supernaturals?'

'Exactly. So that's what she'll be doing. I've no doubt she had people selected before she took you from your cell, and now I bet she's deciding on the final group while we chat in here.' She dragged at the metal around her neck. 'And I hope she gets this off sooner rather than later. It doesn't half itch, and the more I scratch at it, the more I think the bomb might go off.'

I placed my hand on her arm. 'Then stop grabbing at it.' I pulled the shirt away at her throat and peered at the gap between the silver and her flesh. Was there something under her skin? 'Can you feel anything there?'

'No, not really, but I've had this on since I woke up, and it's hard to tell with a thick piece of metal pushed up against your skin.'

I hauled her from the trolley and sat both of us on the bed.

'What happened to you after I teleported into the bunker? When I got outside, there were bodies everywhere, but no sign of you.'

'It was carnage, Cassie. They knew something was going on inside the bunker as red lights and sirens were flashing and screaming as soon as I arrived. I saw about half a dozen of them running to the entrance, demons in human flesh and heavily armed. So I had to stop them getting to you.'

I lifted my hand and touched the scars on her face. 'Is this how you got these and the broken tooth? I thought vampires could heal.'

'We can, as long as we drink enough. But after I slaughtered those guards, someone whacked me on the head as I tried to get into the bunker to help you.' She glanced around the room. 'And you know the rest.' She touched her cheeks. 'These will heal once I've drunk all that blood.' She prodded at her teeth. 'Then I'll be back to my beautiful self.'

We laughed together.

'Thank goodness,' I said.

'But that's why I won't leave you again, Cassie. I don't care who Erasmus picks to go into the Zone, but I'll be by your side.'

'Do you trust her or anyone else here?'

Claudia shook her head. 'Of course not. But I trust you.' She wiped the blood from her top lip, and the smell of it jumped into my throat and tickled at something lurking down there. 'I guess you prevented a nuclear war, then.'

I nodded. 'But I had to kill the president to do it.' I assumed there were hidden cameras in the room recording the conversation, but I didn't care.

'I thought so,' Claudia said. 'They haven't stopped questioning me since I woke here, but they wouldn't tell me what had happened inside the bunker.'

As she spoke, someone knocked on the wall behind us. I turned and tried to remember where the door was.

'Come in.'

The gap opened and a white-uniformed, bespectacled woman in her thirties walked in. Her long, dark hair was fixed into a ponytail, jumping around at the back of her head as she approached. She took a pouch from her pocket.

'I'm here to remove the manacle.'

She came towards us as we got off the bed. Claudia picked blood from her teeth and grinned at the technician.

'Are you taking the explosive out as well?' The thought of it made me scratch my throat.

The woman had a mini screwdriver in her hand. 'That's nothing to do with me.'

I glanced at Claudia. 'But you know about it, right? They wouldn't have sent you here without telling you there's a bomb in her flesh close to where you'll be working.'

She ignored me and sat next to Claudia; it wasn't how I

expected bomb disposal to go. As the unknown woman – she had no name badge – examined the manacle, my vampire friend returned the favour and peered at the human neck pulsing next to her. In one terrifying instant, I imagined Claudia reaching across and ripping the woman's throat out.

The technician spoke to me. 'Step back towards the wall.'

I didn't do that. 'How far is the blast range?'

She glanced around the room.

'Yes, you're right. I don't believe you'll be safer over there if this goes wrong.'

Claudia grinned at me. 'Hell of a way to go, though, don't you think, Cassie?'

I watched the woman place one hand on the manacle and lift it. 'There's a release mechanism under here somewhere.'

My heartbeat increased as Claudia sat still on the bed. 'How many of these have you removed before?'

She kept hold of the metal as she looked at me. 'This is my first.'

Great. 'Who normally does them?'

The screwdriver was in her hand as she paused. 'We don't get many removal requests, to be honest.' She placed the tip of the tool under the manacle. 'I think the guy before me only did three or four.'

'And what happened to him?' Did I really want to know?

'He's no longer with the organisation.'

She moved closer to Claudia's head and I watched my friend's nose twitch. Was it because of the danger or because she smelt the blood pounding inside the human next to her?

'What's your name?' I asked the woman.

Sweat trickled down her forehead as the screwdriver got further under the metal.

'Found it,' she said. Then she turned to me. 'I'm Jennifer, but you can call me Jen.'

Claudia started whistling a familiar tune I struggled to place at first.

'What's that?' I said.

With one hand, she wiped the sweat from Jen's head. 'It's by the Runaways. I worked as a roadie for them once.' She licked the perspiration from her fingers. That's when Jen trembled a little.

'Damn! I nearly had it there.'

I tried to calm her nerves and stop the freight train hurtling towards my heart.

'What are you attempting to do, Jen?'

She paused while Claudia collected more sweat from her head, but she didn't drink it this time. 'There's a small release catch in the middle, but you can't access it with your finger. It's a fiddle getting the screwdriver into the right spot. I might have brought the wrong size.'

Surely this organisation, these Section 25 people weren't all this incompetent? 'Did Dr Erasmus send you here, Jen?'

She glanced at me while trying to find the catch under the manacle. 'Dr Erasmus, no. Commander Bolt ordered me here.'

Okay, so this could be an assassination mission. The question was what to do about it. I could drag her away from Claudia, but that might make her slip and trigger the explosive. Maybe I could talk her down.

'Perhaps you should get the right tool for this, Jen. It's a delicate operation, and we don't want you blowing us all up by accident, do we?'

And then a dark thought consumed my mind. What if this wasn't an accident and Bolt had sent her on a suicide mission? I was ready to knock her hand away from Claudia's neck when the sound of a click came from the metal, and the manacle dropped to the bed.

Claudia's fingers went straight for her throat. 'Christ, I've wanted to scratch that spot for ages.'

There was a look of horror on Jen's face, even more so than when she was fiddling with the screwdriver.

I grabbed Jen's arm. 'Can Claudia set the bomb off by doing that?'

'No, no, I... well, I don't think so. I haven't seen the schematics of the devices inside your kind.'

I pulled her close to me. 'What do you mean by our kind?'

'Supernaturals, I mean supernaturals.'

I pushed her away and touched my throat. 'You people put an explosive in me?'

She stumbled from me and scrambled for the door.

Claudia kicked the manacle at her. 'You can take that back with you since I don't need it anymore.'

Jen left it on the floor and stepped through the gap in the wall before it closed. I went into the bathroom and stared into the mirror, my fingers brushing across my neck: I couldn't feel anything there. Claudia stood next to me, space in the glass where her reflection should have been.

'There's nothing there, Cassie. Maybe they're lying, you know, to force us into doing what they want.'

'I'm not sure. We were unconscious for God knows how long, and they'd need to have some way of controlling us; an internal explosive device seems as good an option as any.'

She leant into me and placed her delicate hand to my throat.

'I can't feel anything there or under my skin. Can you use your Arcane abilities to see if it's inside you?'

Cold air slipped from my mouth and settled over the mirror, and, at that moment, I didn't see myself but Alice. The damage to my ear was gone. All that was there was my sister's disbelieving face through those first few days we were together when she kept bumping into the supernatural and trying to explain it away using science, just as Erasmus had done earlier. The doctor had pretended to be kind to me, to be friendly, but she'd mentioned nothing about an explosive device implanted in my neck. I trusted none of them; it was up to Claudia and me to solve this problem without them.

I turned to her. 'I haven't had those abilities since I woke up here. I've tried many times to use them, but it's useless. Perhaps I used them all up during the attack on the president and his entourage.'

She shook her head. 'No, I don't believe that. Lucy told me your Arcane gifts are inherent, and they will develop and grow as you and your sister get older. I think she helped kick-start them before the fight, and now they're probably lying dormant until something inside you ignites them again.'

I hoped she was right as I led her into the main room. Then I let go of her and checked the clock on the wall; it wouldn't be long before Erasmus returned. I took a sandwich and ate half of it, speaking to Claudia as I did.

'Do you trust Lucy?'

She snatched an apple from the food trolley and bit into it. 'You want to know if I trust the Devil, the Queen of Lies?'

'Yes.' I finished the sarnie and started on a sausage roll.

'Lucy saved my life, Cassie; mine and many others.'

'Including all those she sent to their deaths outside the presidential mansion?'

'I suppose.' She dropped apple peel to the floor. 'Nothing is ever black and white, Cassie, even dealing with the Devil.'

'You've got that right, vampire.'

I turned to the sound of the voice, not seeing Lucy in the room, but Commander Bolt at the door.

The Devil wasn't there, and I didn't know whether to be disappointed or not.

11 ALICE: BELLA

Bullets whizzed past my head, but it wasn't that which bothered me. Bella lay on top of me, pinning my body to the ground.

'What are you doing?' I said.

'I'm saving your life.'

All I saw in the dark was the whiteness of her teeth. She grabbed my arm, rolling us both from the centre of the room and behind a sofa. The lights flickered before a male voice spoke.

And I recognised it.

'I'm only here for the vampire. You're free to leave if you hand her over.'

Bella pressed her lips close to my face. 'The boy has it bad for me. And he's lying. He won't let you go. He can't leave any witnesses.'

I inched my head around to the side, seeing Tom Blaze and two armed men near the lift. There was no sign of Rivers. I slipped back to Bella.

'He's here to take you to the government.'

'No,' she said. 'This is all for him. Whoever he's working

for now, the Nexus is kaput, so I'm guessing this isn't on their orders. I'd be surprised if they know anything about this little operation. He wants me all to himself, the naughty boy.' She appeared to be enjoying herself.

'Why don't you rush over there and take those guns from them?'

She reached behind me, her fingers brushing against my cheek as she removed something from the wall. It was the remains of a wooden bullet.

'One of these in my heart and it's game over.'

'So what do we do?'

'You need to trick him. He's not the brightest bulb in the ceiling.' As she said that, someone turned on the lights.

'You're already wanted by the police, Alice. And now you've murdered Dr Rivers.'

His voice grated on my nerves. The sound of the doctor's wheelchair moved closer to us. When it reached the side of the sofa, Rivers sat slumped in the seat, her body covered in blood. I had no love for the woman, but she'd deserved better than that.

I turned to Bella.

'If I get you out of here alive, will you promise to help me find your brother and my mother?'

She stared at me with something close to admiration.

'So it's me you're striking a bargain with?'

'Do we have a deal?'

Bella shrugged. 'Why not? I like adventure, and I sense lots of those are forthcoming for you, Alice Arcane. I promise to help you find your mother and my brother.'

'How do I know I can trust you?'

'What choice do you have?'

She was right.

'You have two minutes to comply,' Tom Blaze shouted.

'It's now or never, Alice.' Our bodies were close together as she held out her hand. I shook it without hesitation.

'You were right about him not being the brightest.'

'What do you mean?'

I arched my head towards the dead doctor in her wheelchair.

'He sent us a weapon. All you have to do is return it to him.'

Bella grinned like an exploding sun, her fingers on the bottom of the wheelchair in a flash. Then she was up and hurling it towards Tom Blaze and his goons. I followed her, somewhat slower, but quickly enough to see Dr Ellen Rivers perform her last helpful function in this life. Her body and the wheelchair hit our assailants together, the three of them crumpling to the ground as one. Bella skimmed across the floor like a pebble bouncing off a lake. I stumbled behind her as the double crack of broken necks splintered the room.

It was two more pointless deaths. 'You shouldn't have done that,' I said.

I was surprised to see the remorse on her face. 'You're right. I should have drained them first. I haven't had a drink for such a long time, and this little escapade has exhausted me. Still, I can always feast on him.'

She turned her attention to Blaze, pinned under his former boss and her wheelchair.

'My legs are broken,' he cried.

Bella bent and stroked his hair. 'That will soon be the least of your problems, Thomas.' Pure evil dripped from her. My arm was on her shoulder before I knew what I was doing.

'Leave him alone. He can't harm us.'

She twisted her head to glare at me, her face the horrifying vision of vampires from everyone's nightmares. Her eyes burned yellow and red, while her teeth were sharpened daggers ready to bite.

'No, but he can be useful. I can't find my brother and your mother unless I'm at full strength, and I require blood for that.'

'Not his.' My defiance matched her venom.

'We need blood, me and you.'

'What?'

'Please help me,' Blaze pleaded on the floor as I moved away.

Bella continued, 'As I mentioned, I'm useless to you like this. I have to be strong again, and that will only return once I've drunk. Plus,' she stepped over Blaze's head, 'I've been meditating on what you told me about Lucy training you and Cassie in your nascent Arcane abilities. Lucy tricked you, but not in the way you said.'

'What do you mean?'

'In case you haven't realised by now, everything in the supernatural world is based on sustenance.'

'Every living thing needs to feed to survive.'

'Exactly, and for creatures like us, it's either devouring the soul or blood. So I think when the Queen of Lies trained you and your sister, she was secretly feeding both of you some of her blood: the blood of an archangel, more for Cassie than you to deceive and control you.'

The image of Lucy slipping her blood into me made me sick.

'How would that work?'

'Because of your specific heritage, your unique blood-line, you must require unique blood to fuel your abilities. The Nephilim lineage is human and angel; yours, from what you told me, appears to be Nephilim and archangel, which is why Lucy's blood, fed to you without your knowledge, ignited your gifts. And that's why we both need blood to be who we truly are.'

I looked around the depleted Nexus. 'Even if what you say is true, I don't see many angels, fallen or otherwise, to help me here.'

'We can assist each other.' She took hold of my hand and led us from the moaning young man. 'I want blood, but you won't let me feed on these humans.' She gave a cursory glance to Tom Blaze. 'To get your mother and sister back, you need access to your Arcane powers, so you require angel blood, and you'll have a hard time finding that. The answer to both our problems is the same thing: demon blood.'

My guts churned at the thought of it. 'Demon blood?'

'Absolutely. Didn't you know the First of the Fallen created her demon army from her own archangel blood? God had Their children, angels and humans, so Lucy wanted her own. That's why we have demons now.'

'How... how did she do that?'

'No one knows. It's a secret like Coke or the mixture for proper Yorkshire puddings. There have been plenty of imitators, but there's only one real thing.' She rubbed at her chin. 'Like Elvis or Bowie.'

My head spun with the idea of Lucy's blood and demon blood accelerating my so-called Arcane abilities. But it had to be true; that's why they worked so well for Cassie during Lucy's training, because the Queen of Hell held back with me, but went full throttle with my sister. That must have been why my abilities reappeared when the vampires had me trapped, because I tasted their blood.

The chorus from *Life on Mars* echoed around inside my head.

'How come you know of Elvis and Bowie if you've been imprisoned since the 1940s?'

She nodded at Blaze as he sobbed on the floor. 'I told you: Tommy paid me plenty of visits unknown to the others, and he was always desperate to introduce me to the things he loved the most. I'll say this for the boy: he had great taste in music.'

I ignored the way she spoke of him in the past tense.

'Okay.' I swept the sweat from my head. 'You're saying if I drink demon blood, it will provide me access to the powers I had before: teleportation, telekinesis, flying, invisibility and telepathy?'

'That or it'll kill you.'

'Great. I'll give it a miss then. But demon blood will return your strength to you?'

'Not only that, but it will aid me in locating my brother, which will help you find your mother.'

'How does that work?'

'Dracula and I have always had a connection, a familial bond there before we became vampires. But I haven't seen him in decades, and my imprisonment, as I've already told you, has weakened me, so I'm like a new baby. However, a barrel of demon blood will soon get me back to fighting fitness, and I'll have a good idea of where my little brother is hiding.'

That was all I needed to hear. I strode over to Tom Blaze and moved the obstruction from him. His legs were crushed and bleeding badly.

Tears filled his eyes. 'You can't leave me like this, Alice.'

I went to Ellen Rivers's corpse and grabbed her blanket. I took my blade and cut it into two and used the bits as makeshift tourniquets. Then I searched through his pockets for his phone and car keys.

I peered into his defeated face.

'Do your superiors know you're here?'

He struggled to speak. 'No. This is all on me.'

Bella shot me a look of I told you so.

'I'll call for an ambulance when we're outside. Where's your vehicle?'

'Thank you, Alice. Take the lift to the top floor. You'll exit out of the main door through a gift shop. There's a jeep there.'

I turned to Bella. 'Are you coming?'

She gave Tom a last lingering grin before joining me.

'So, what's the plan, boss?'

The metal moved up with a clang and throttle as I clasped the keys in my hand.

'You need to drink, so we'll get you some demon blood.'

'And for you?'

'You said it could kill me.'

She threw her hands in the air as the lift crawled to a stop.

'It's all hypothetical, Alice. Are you risk-averse?'

'I'm here with you, so what do you think?'

'I believe this is the beginning of a beautiful friendship.' She winked at me. 'A child of the Arcane and the Queen of the Vampires. What could go wrong?'

The door opened and I peered into the daytime. I turned to her.

'Can you walk in the sunlight?' I had one foot outside.

'Normally, yes, but I'm weak from lack of blood.' She turned her face from the light. 'Give me your jacket, so I don't burst into flames.'

I did as she requested and she placed it over her head.

'I'll find the car.' I went out and looked at the tourists. Bella took a tentative step behind me. If my jacket slipped from her face, would all be lost? I pointed the keys into the crowd of cars and pressed the button. A beep and two clicks drew my gaze to the left. I strode towards the vehicle without a thought for Bella and her safety, which was stupid, considering how much I needed her.

A group of kids ran in front of me and shouted something I couldn't make out. I told them to call an ambulance for Blaze. At least the sun being out meant the tide hadn't come in yet and we wouldn't be stranded on the island.

I opened the door and got into the jeep.

Bella was next to me with her head covered.

'Can you drive?'

'Probably better than you.'

She tapped her hands on the dashboard. 'I met Henry Ford once, such a horrible man. It's funny how people like me are called monsters, but he was as evil as they came.' She leant towards me as I started the engine. 'I guess only humans can get away with such terrible things.'

I spun the wheel and pulled the car out of its parking spot.

'I don't care about any of that. I'll get you your demons, and then you've got to find your brother.'

'You're the boss, Alice. Can we have some music while we drive?'

I turned the radio on and skimmed through the channels. I settled on a station playing dance tunes as we headed towards Newcastle. The thought of demons and discos reverberated around my skull as Bella sank into the passenger seat and pulled my jacket over her face. I puffed out my cheeks and let out a breath of hot air.

While we drove, I considered whether I'd drink demon blood and risk my life to find my family.

And if I trusted the vampire next to me.

12 CASSIE: OMEGA

Dr Erasmus pushed past Bolt, shoving a pen and paper towards me.

'This is our agreement, our contract with the two of you, promising safe passage from Section 25 on your successful return from the Zone with President Dixon.'

'You didn't say I had to get him out, but go in to try and save him.'

Bolt snorted laughter. 'You think we'd trust you in there without the proper motivation?' He glared at me. 'If you can't retrieve Dixon alive, then don't bother leaving the Zone.'

Claudia dropped an empty blood bag to the floor, the top of her mouth and lips looking as if she'd smeared thick, moist lipstick across them.

'Speaking of proper motivation, when are you going to take these bombs out of our necks?'

She moved towards him as if about to pounce. As she did, two armed guards bundled their way into the room. Claudia was only a few feet from the commander.

He smirked at her. 'There are wooden bullets dipped in Holy Water and garlic in those weapons, vampire.'

She flicked a hand at him before jumping back to the bed in fits of laughter. She grabbed her stomach and rolled on the covers. It took her a good minute to regain control. Then she grinned at him.

'Oh, Commander Bolt, if that's the level of knowledge you have in this new supernatural-busting organisation of yours, then I fear you won't last long.' She flexed her legs and stood to her entire five foot two height. 'Actually, I don't fear it at all.'

Erasmus stepped between the soldiers and the bed. 'Those weapons won't hurt you?'

Claudia stared past her and at me. 'Do you trust these people to send us into a deadly blue dust cloud?'

I took the paper and pen from Erasmus and twisted her around. The soldiers got jumpy and raised their guns at me.

'Put those down,' the doctor said to them.

They looked to Bolt for confirmation, and he nodded. I placed the paper against her back, pushed the pen down as hard as possible, and signed both copies. Then I turned her around and gave her one copy, but kept the pen. She didn't ask for it, so I slipped it into my pocket before someone noticed. I held the contract in front of me.

'Is this binding in a court of law?'

Bolt did that disgusting snorting thing again while Erasmus scowled at him.

'It is, and you have my word, both of you, of safe passage out of America once you return President Dixon to us.' She turned to Claudia. 'Now explain to me why those bullets won't hurt you.'

Claudia snatched the paper from my hand and scanned through it, talking all the time as she did.

'I once worked as a contract lawyer for Abe Lincoln.' She glanced at the soldiers. 'It's terrible what you people did to him.'

Commander Bolt shook his head. 'How old are you, girl; fifteen?'

She folded the paper and slipped it into her pocket.

'I'll have you know I had my sixteenth birthday,' she stuck out her hand and pretended to look at a watch she didn't have, 'oh, at least two hundred years ago.'

'Tell me about the bullets, Claudia,' Erasmus said.

My vampire friend was close enough to the doctor she could have snapped her neck with one flick of her slight teenage wrist.

'Holy Water and garlic are fairy tales for the fiction brigade and nerdy boys.' She smirked at Bolt. 'You're wasting time dipping your ammo in those substances, Bolty Boy.'

He growled at her, 'You lie. We've used them on other vampires, and they've worked perfectly.'

Claudia pulled a curious face at him. 'Really? Are you sure? What happened?'

He stuck out his chest. 'That's classified information.'

She looked at me and laughed. 'Okay, then. When do we get this show on the road?'

'We need to go to the briefing. Follow me.' Erasmus left the room, so we strode after her. Bolt and his goons marched behind us at a safe distance.

Claudia leant into me as we moved. 'That was nonsense what he said about the Holy Water and garlic. They don't do fig to a vampire. I should know; I've eaten and drunk both many times.'

'You think he's lying?'

'He could be, I suppose, but what would be the point?

It's more likely he's just as stupid as the rest of them in this Section 25 gang. Perhaps you killed all the intelligent people in that bunker.'

'I got the impression earlier he doesn't believe in the supernatural.'

Claudia put her hand over her mouth and whispered to me, 'Then he's in for a rude awakening sooner rather than later.'

We followed Erasmus along the corridor. The soldiers kept a steady pace behind as I considered methods of escape. And then I thought of the town and how much responsibility would be mine if I left those people to die. I was so busy thinking about it, I didn't realise Erasmus had stopped walking and I bumped into her.

'Damn!' I prodded my nose into her back, and her thin frame was harder than I expected, resulting in a shooting pain running through my face. Erasmus looked at me without flinching. Then she opened another hole in the wall, and we stepped into a vast room similar to the one with all the screens. There was a large table and chairs, plus half a dozen armed security guards and three white-uniformed blokes, who I assumed were scientists like Erasmus. She pointed to the far side of the table.

'Meet the rest of your team.'

I stared at them, five individuals who looked as pleased to be there as I was.

Claudia stepped forward and presented an extravagant curtsy. 'Charmed, I'm sure.'

His two grunts flanked Bolt. 'Let's get on with this, Erasmus. The plane is waiting to take Omega Team to the Zone.'

I glanced at the digital clock on all the monitors. 'Don't we have more than ten hours to get there?' Before any of them replied, I fired off a second question. 'If we're the Omega Team, what happened to Alpha?'

Erasmus answered before Bolt could open his square mouth. 'The Zone has picked up pace in the last hour; it will be over the town by midnight.' The clock was at 8pm. 'And Alpha Team was the first group we sent in.'

'The ones who never came out?' Claudia said.

'Indeed, and now time is of the essence. We've got thirty minutes to agree on the plan once we get the introductions out of the way.'

So she introduced Omega Team to each other. There were six Special Forces operatives under the leadership of Captain Grant Hall, a tall man with a winning smile who was obviously under strict instructions from Commander Bolt. Then there were us, the supernaturals: she presented Claudia and me, and then the other five who made up the non-human contingent of this rescue mission.

First up was Colleen, an Irish redhead with eyes to match her mane. She was a banshee, there to provide sonic muscle if other avenues didn't work against the hostile forces inside the Zone. Sayan, a thirty-year-old woman, was next: a Siberian shaman, adding some mysticism to our group. Then we had Wovoka, a Native American medicine man and expert in the Ghost Dance, whatever that was. The most interesting one was Luke, the Harlem Dust Devil, who could control certain elements. Hopefully, he'd be able to keep the blue mist away from us. Finally, there was a seven-foot-tall rake-thin bloke named Allister. I wondered what his purpose was until he stepped near to me and I saw the purple in his pupils. I slammed my hand on the desk hard enough to make a few of the white-uniformed bodies flinch.

'We're not taking a demon with us.'

When Allister grinned, there was a purple shimmer between his teeth. Erasmus placed her hands on the table.

'We need him, Cassie; he knows what the Zone is.'

I counted slowly inside my head, waiting for my heart to slow down to something near to normal. Then I moved towards him.

'Every demon I've met has tried to kill me; what makes you so different?'

He crossed his legs as his smirk grew broader and brighter. 'I don't even know who you are, child.' He glanced at Bolt and the armed troops in the room. 'If I hadn't been betrayed, I wouldn't be here.' He lifted his arm and flicked his fingers at me. 'I have no interest in you or any of these others.' He glared at Erasmus. 'My job is to get you inside what you call the Zone, and then you can do whatever you want.'

Erasmus removed her digital device and placed it on the table. 'You don't leave until I say so, Allister.' He peered at the device as if he wanted to devour it. I grabbed his arm and turned him towards me.

'What do you know about the blue cloud?'

He shook his head and laughed as he twisted from my grip.

'It's not a cloud, you silly girl. That which you call the Zone is a physical manifestation of an ancient deity known as Pandora.'

'Pandora from the Greek myth?' Claudia said.

Allister shrugged. 'Probably. All I know is she was banished to another realm thousands of years ago, and now she's found a gap somewhere to push her tendrils into this world; the blue mist is her gathering strength to break through completely. And when she does, she'll bring a whole dimension of horror with her.'

Erasmus made notes on her device. 'How is she gathering strength?'

The demon laughed. 'How do you think? She's feeding.'

I asked the question I didn't want to hear the answer to. 'What's she feeding on?'

He shook his head. 'Pandora is devouring whoever is unfortunate enough to still be in that town.' He turned to Bolt. 'What did you say its name is, Valhalla?' The demon snorted again. 'That seems appropriate.'

'How do we stop her?' I said.

He held up his hands. 'Your guess is as good as mine.'

'How was she exiled the first time?'

Wovoka stepped forward. 'Once inside the blue mist, I'll perform the Ghost Dance and enter the Spirit World to speak to those who banished this creature millennia ago, and then we'll have the answers.'

He was impressive in his words, and only when I looked closer did I realise he was older than I first thought. Initially, during the introduction, he appeared to be of similar age to the others, in his thirties, but now he seemed twice that.

'Okay, let's lay out our strategy.' Bolt took charge and nodded to Captain Hall. For someone disbelieving of the supernatural, he'd accepted this Omega Team pretty quickly.

He turned the big screen on and pointed at the map: it was of the town, with points showing where we'd enter and the last known position of President Dixon. As Hall described the plan, I glanced at Erasmus and wondered if I'd underestimated her. She'd gathered together the demon with knowledge of what we faced, the medicine man to find our enemy's weakness, a dust devil to control the mist, a banshee for sonic muscle, and me because of my exploits in killing the last president; but why the shaman? What could she bring to this operation?

Then there was Claudia.

I sidled up to her as Hall droned on, whispering in her ear as the captain handed everyone a small communications device and earpiece.

'You needn't go, Claudia. We've got enough with the rest of the team.'

She took an earpiece and communicator and gave me mine. I watched as the others pinned them to their clothes, and then did the same.

'You won't get rid of me that easily, Cassie.' She placed the small plastic into her ear. 'I just hope they play some decent music when we go into battle.'

I attached the communicator to my shirt collar and plugged the piece into my ear.

'Music?'

'You know, like that bit in *Apocalypse Now*, though I'd prefer something more modern – maybe *Paint It Black*.'

It was only as we went to leave the room that I realised this was the first part of the building which wasn't wholly white: it was red.

Then the red door opened for us.

13 ALICE: NEWCASTLE

The journey to Newcastle took less than an hour. I avoided the military patrols and was lucky to find a parking spot near our destination. Bella had slumbered all the way there, her face protected from the sun by the dark glasses and one of the baseball caps I'd found in the glove compartment. Thomas Blaze had been kind enough to leave that combination for me, too. As we sat in the car, we looked like victims of terrible plastic surgery.

She pushed the sunglasses up on her nose. 'What is this place you've brought me to?'

'The building across the road is a police station.'

She gave me a Hollywood smile. 'Have you reconsidered giving yourself up?'

'There are demons in there, including the local Demon Lord.'

Bella lifted her shades to peer at me. 'I admire your ambition, Alice. Will you tell me how you know this?'

'Cassie and I were taken here, and then interrogated by the Demon Lord Aziz in his guise as a police officer before he instructed his cronies to bury my sister and me alive in Tynemouth Priory.'

Bella's eyes narrowed as she scrutinised me, and for a second, I glanced at centuries of knowledge burning inside her.

'You've been on some journey since I saw you last.' She gazed out the side window. 'We've got time to kill before the sun goes down, so we might as well get to know each other better now we're partners.' Bella twisted her body around to turn to me. 'You should tell me everything that happened after you left the Nexus the first time, not just what you told me a few hours ago. Leave out none of the gory details.'

I sat there, looking through my sunglasses at her and contemplating her notion of partnership. Lucy had claimed to be my partner and had let me down, so how could I trust Bella? The only person I trusted was Cassie, and I had no idea where she was.

'I told you most of it earlier. How did you know my mother was the last of the Nephilim?'

Bella squeezed her knees next to mine. 'Thomas was a fountain of knowledge. When he wasn't trying to impress me with what was on the internet, he was spilling every Nexus secret he knew. After you escaped from Rivers and her murderous mechanical legs, word spread like wildfire around the supernatural world regarding your exploits. The last of the Nephilim and her offspring, the Children of the Arcane, could only be about you and your sister. Poor Thomas was not best pleased. It took all of my charms to calm him down.'

'What did he want from you?'

The glint in her eye was bright enough to sparkle behind the darkness of the glasses.

'Guess?'

'Sex?'

Bella burst out laughing. 'There was not much I could do about that when permanently pinned to a wall. No, he wanted what everybody needs: love and a connection with a like-minded soul. Haven't you been searching for that all your life?'

I scratched at my arm until my skin turned red. 'You know I'm only sixteen years old?'

Bella removed her shades. 'If we're to have this conversation, we need to see each other's eyes.'

I removed my glasses. 'Okay. We might as well make it interesting while killing time.' I also hoped I'd learn more about her, whether I could trust her, not only through her words, but by examining her face and body language.

'It all starts at an early age, Alice. Childhood is the most crucial part of anyone's life, human or supernatural.' That burning experience now seemed to tremble inside her pupils. 'A child's formative years, the bonds they create with their parents and their first learning experiences, deeply affect their future physical, cognitive, emotional and social development. For a parent, the failure to see the world from their child's perspective can have several negative consequences.'

'Was it like that for you?'

Bella smiled at me. 'Do you want to hear the story of my life?'

'Will you tell me about you and your brother, how you became vampires?'

She tossed the glasses forward so they clattered against the windscreen.

'We were never friends, but we weren't rivals either. I'm a year older than him, but he was still the heir to our father's fortune, lands, and title. Do you know why that was?'

'Because you're female, and he's male.'

A flush of anger glimmered on Bella's cheekbones. 'Which meant I was less than nothing in our family line, just something to be used as a bargaining chip in future deals with others of wealth and privilege.' The tension in the car increased as she spoke. 'On my thirteenth birthday, I was promised in marriage to a local nobleman, a man three times my age. I was impetuous then and refused, so my father beat me until the bruises covered my stomach and back. He never touched my face, of course.'

I clutched at my chest, fearful to hear more, but also needing to listen to her. And I think she was desperate to tell me.

'You were married at thirteen?'

The smile crept over her face. 'No, my prospective husband had an unfortunate accident the night before the wedding. He fell from the wall of the castle and crushed his skull on the ground.' Bella ran her tongue across the top of her lip. 'There was talk of his head injury happening before the fall and he'd been pushed over the wall, but nothing could be proved. His family wailed about it, of course, but they couldn't do anything but return to their lands to mourn.' She glanced at her hands as if she was still in that night centuries ago. 'After that, strangely enough, no other noble suitors presented themselves to my father for my hand in marriage.

'A few years later, my father's soldiers caught a vampire terrorising the villages around our castle. It gave him a great idea on how to test which of us was the more resourceful between my brother and me.'

'Resourceful?'

'I'd spent years telling everyone how much smarter I was than my brother and had proved it many times. It was my way of showing him and others I should be the rightful heir to our power, regardless of my sex. So my father gave us both the ultimate test.' The smile shrank from her. 'And perhaps it was punishment for me.'

My heart thumped against my ribs. 'He put the two of you in a room with the vamp?'

'It was a game for him and his friends to watch. We had weapons and they'd weakened the vampire through beatings and starvations, but it wasn't enough.'

'What happened?' Against my better judgement, I felt sorry for her.

'My brother swung his sword and chopped off the vampire's arm, but he was overconfident and arrogant. He turned to our father in triumph, ready to receive all the praise and accolades. The vampire was on him in seconds, his teeth tearing into my brother's throat. I could have stopped him. I knew all I had to do was decapitate the creature, and it would all have been over. I'd be the hero of the hour and would have proved myself better than my brother. But I didn't.'

'You wanted to be free of your father?'

'As blood dripped from the vampire's mouth and across my brother's face, I promised myself I'd let no one else control me ever again.'

'What did you do?'

'I knelt next to the creature and told him if he turned me into a thing like him, I'd help him escape.'

'Is that what you did?'

'In a fashion. I allowed the vampire to take me hostage, for him to barter his release by letting me live.'

'And your father agreed to it?'

Bella laughed. 'No, he didn't care about me. But my brother lay choking at my feet with vampire blood filling his mouth. So dear Papa panicked, letting the vamp drag me away as his people tried to save my brother's life.

'I fled the castle and my family. My brother inherited our name and lands and went his own way. I don't know what happened to the vampire who made us. He dumped me in the forest after taking my blood and infecting me with his.'

'He abandoned you there?'

'I guess he didn't want to linger near my father's castle, and who could blame him? I felt the same way.'

As the modern world passed us by outside, all I could see was a younger Bella on her own in the trees centuries past.

'How old were you then?'

She glanced at her fingers. 'It's so long ago, I can barely remember.' She looked back at me. 'About twenty-four, I think.'

'A bit older than me.'

She grinned. 'I guess so.'

A young girl walked past the car and peered at me through the window. She had braces on her teeth and wore glasses as thick as a telescope. I imagined her looking deep inside me and finding nothing human.

'What did you do after the vampire left you in the forest?'

A wistful look crossed Bella's face. 'I'm not sure how long it took me to die, and then come back, but my father didn't send anyone to search for me because they'd have found me if he had.' Her gaze peered right into me. 'Or perhaps they did, and they abandoned me there, anyway.' She smiled again. 'I remember waking and stinking of blood and mud with a constant ache running through all of me. I knew what I was then, that the vampire had kept his promise.'

'Did you see your brother after that?'

'Our paths crossed on occasion, but he was obsessed with creating his legend across the world.'

'What does that mean?'

'He found some Irish writer and spun him a tale of Dracula, the great vampire. He became famous, and the rest of us had to be more careful about stepping out of the shadows. I'm convinced he did it to get back at me.'

'Are you saying Stoker's book was dictated to him by your brother?'

'I think it was more of an interview, but it was, ultimately, an exercise in narcissism.'

I raised a hand to my mouth and coughed. 'Well, I don't believe he's been happy with the results for some while.' I told her about Dracula's fifty-year self-imposed exile and how we'd awakened him in his house in Whitby.

Bella shook her head. 'I accepted our isolated childhood and lack of love, but he always struggled with the loneliness and emptiness. This is why he's taken your mother.'

I shuddered at the thought of it. I removed the paper from my pocket and placed it on the dashboard to get the idea from my mind.

Bella's eyes widened. 'Did you steal that from Rivers?'

'She gave it to me.' I opened it to expose the coded figures printed on it. 'Were you a German spy during the war? Is that why you were in the Tube station in 1940?'

Bella picked it up and ran her fingers over the symbols. A deep echoing sadness seeped from her eyes.

'My one regret is not killing that man when I had the chance.'

'Which man?'

'Hitler. I met him and the rest of his criminal gang at a party thrown by Leni Riefenstahl in 1936.' She brushed her hand across her face, and it came away damp. 'It was decades after the war when I learnt about the Holocaust. Thomas was teaching me history using the internet.' She let out a small breath of air. 'I was in the same room as them: Hitler, Himmler, Goering, Goebbels, Hess, Speer, and others. It would have been child's play to kill them all there and then.'

'Why were you there?'

The spark returned to her eyes as she stared at me. 'You were right; I was a spy, but not for the Nazis. I was working for Winnie.'

'Churchill!' I was gobsmacked.

'I'd known him since the end of the Boer War. He had his faults, like all of us, but my God, he was entertaining. I was in Berlin during most of the 1920s and 1930s and he asked me to keep him updated on what was happening. I left in 36.' Regret was written all over her face.

'Did he know what you are?'

'A vampire? Yes, he knew. The supernatural was no surprise to him. I was working for him again in 1940 when that bomb went off, and the debris punctured my heart in the Tube station. I could almost appreciate the irony of it.'

'What were you doing in London? Why didn't Churchill rescue you?'

Bella held the coded message in her hand. 'One of Winnie's secret agents had intercepted other messages before this one.' She peered straight into my eyes. 'The Nazis took the supernatural much more seriously than other governments; they even had an organisation dedicated to it. Once the war started, they poured more resources into it than the Allies realised. Then the rumour spread they'd weaponised it to use in the war.'

'Weaponised the supernatural? How?'

'Apparently, one of their experiments was to create a supernatural super-soldier. And they sent it to London in 1940. That's what I was looking for in the Tube.'

'When the authorities discovered you, why did you end up in the Nexus?'

'The only person who knew about my mission was Churchill, and no one would inform the prime minister about a body in a Tube station. I found out later, thanks again to Thomas, that the disaster at Balham Station was kept from the British public for years.'

'You could have informed the Nexus you were working for Churchill the first time they removed the stake from you.'

Bella laughed. 'I did, or at least I told them about my relationship with Winnie. But, with the madness of the war and the disorganisation of the Nexus, they didn't pull the wood from my heart until 1960. And no one believed me about Churchill then.'

I took the paper from her and studied the code again.

'Do you think this Nazi supernatural creature is still alive?'

She stroked her chin. 'Anything is possible. We can look for it once we've finished here, if you like?'

'Let's find your brother and my mother first.' I opened the car door.

'Where are you going?'

'I need something to eat. You stay here and keep your head down. I'll return soon enough.'

'I thought you had no money?'

'There was twenty quid in the glove compartment with the glasses and hats.'

'Thomas was always very thoughtful.' She leant towards me. 'Make sure no one recognises you, Alice.'

I closed the door and stepped around the corner. It took under two minutes to find a shop, where I bought a vegetarian pie and a bag of crisps. There was a church nearby, so I went there and sat on a bench outside to eat. But, unfortunately, the gloom which would protect Bella was still a few hours away.

Was what she'd told me of her life the truth? I was feeling sorry for her, so I must have believed it.

But could I trust her?

I bit into a piece of potato and stared at the statue of an angel opposite me.

What choice did I have?

And how much more would it take before I found my family?

14 CASSIE: THE PLANE

Twenty minutes later, we marched towards a military plane. Claudia was at my side as we strode across the tarmac.

'We could make a run for it now.'

I scanned the area in every direction, seeing nothing but desert for miles.

'The odds aren't in our favour, Claudia.'

Plus, we had six heavily armed Special Forces operatives with us, and I knew Bolt and his regular goons were watching. So I didn't fancy our chances.

She had a quick look and came to the same conclusion.

'You're right. Maybe when we're in the air. We overpower them in the plane and take control, tell them to fly us wherever we want.' We were a hundred yards from the aircraft. 'Or we get the shaman to magic us out of there.' It was tempting, but the chill of the night bit me back into reality.

And I had other responsibilities now.

'I won't abandon thousands of people to be consumed by an ancient monster, Claudia.'

'You're going to kill this Pandora?'

'I will, but only if I have to.'

Erasmus gave a final pep talk before we boarded as she handed Hall her communication device.

'This is your ultimate motivation before you leave.'

She nodded to him and he pressed on the screen. The lights in our necks lit up, seven red dots flickering in the dark, but I felt it before that, a faint, warm tickling sensation at the throat. I placed my fingers there as a light hum travelled into my ears and head.

I glared at her.

'You don't trust us?' Those ruby spots blinked in the surrounding night.

'It's just a little insurance policy, Cassie.' She glanced at the rest of my comrades. 'And don't think to overwhelm Captain Hall to get the trigger.' She patted her breast pocket. 'I can do it from here.'

'You need to work on your motivational speeches, Olivia,' Claudia said as we entered the plane. The last thing I saw before the door closed was Erasmus speaking into a concealed microphone.

It was enormous inside, room enough to squeeze in a decent array of equipment and weapons, but there were only thirteen of us there. That number wasn't lost on the demon.

'I hope none of you is superstitious.'

His grin lightened up the gloom and tempted me to punch him in the head. Maybe I'd get the chance when this was all over. I touched the little-death hiding in my neck as we shuffled along to the bottom of the carriage. Hall and his Special Forces team stuck close to the front and kept their distance. The demon, medicine man, shaman and the banshee sat opposite me, Claudia and the dust devil. There were no announcements as the plane started and picked up speed on the runway.

Colleen was the first to buckle up. 'I hate flying.'

Her faint Irish twang reminded me of a Roddy Doyle movie I'd seen a few years ago. Her flame-red hair hung down to her shoulders, and I pictured her on a stage somewhere belting out tunes, halfway between Patti Smith and Diana Ross. Our ride accelerated, and then lifted into the air. We were all strapped in then, apart from Claudia, so I pointed at her belt.

'Oh, I don't need it. Turbulence doesn't bother me. I have perfect balance. Watch.'

With all eyes on her, she crossed her legs and floated three feet above the rest of us while whistling the theme tune from *Top Gun*. The shaman and medicine man gazed at her before engaging in whispered conversation. How many of them had known each other before this? I glanced up at my hovering friend.

'Don't hurt yourself.'

She wiggled her nose at me. 'I'm fine. From up here, we look like *The Magnificent Seven*.'

'Didn't most of them die?'

The dust devil leant towards me. 'I've always preferred the *Seven Samurai*.'

Claudia dropped back into her seat. 'I met Kurosawa once, you know. He was a very nice man. I helped him get funding for *The Hidden Fortress*.' She crossed her legs. 'I love that movie.'

Colleen fumbled into her pocket and removed a packet of cigarettes and a lighter.

'I need a drag.'

'How did you find those in the pokey?' Claudia asked her.

The banshee took one from the pack. 'I have friends in high places.' The plane rose as she spoke. I pushed closer to her.

'You can't light that in here.'

She flicked at the lighter. 'Why not? Most of us will die, anyway.' She put the flame on the cigarette and it fizzled into life.

I controlled my temper. 'Because it stinks, and I hate the smoke.'

She took a drag and pouted at me. 'Poor baby girl, do you have asthma?'

I was about to snatch it from her when it burst into pieces and dropped to her knee. She yelped as she fumbled at the scorch mark on her trouser leg, hitting herself to put it out. The dead stub fell to the floor.

'What the? Which one of you did that?'

'It was me.'

We all turned to the dust devil. Even Hall and his troops watched as Luke held his hands up. His fingers shimmered and vibrated as particles moved in the surrounding air. I think we were all impressed with the show, apart from Colleen.

'I'll rip your throat out for that, Yank.' Her trouser leg continued to smoke as she unbuckled and made to reach for the dust devil. Before she could, he lifted one vibrating hand towards her and the red at her neck came vibrantly alive. 'Fuck!' It was an Irish expletive, but I guessed we all thought it.

Captain Hall covered the distance between the two groups in record time.

'Stop that.'

But Luke ignored him. Then the red lights flickered awake on the others opposite us. I reached for my throat, but my skin was cold. I leant across Claudia and touched Luke's arm.

'How are you doing this?'

He turned to me as his hand continued to shimmer. 'I can control particles in the air and, regardless of my name, not just dust. These devices they implanted into our necks likely got bits of dirt inside them during construction. So all I'm doing is tickling them a little.'

Hall pulled on the trigger and pointed the gun at Luke's face.

'Stop it now, or I'll blow your head off.'

Luke only smiled, saying nothing. It was up to me to speak.

'If you do that, you'll kill us all, Captain. Once Luke loses control, then all four bombs will detonate and probably activate the ones in us. No one here will survive. So put the weapon away.'

He didn't look at me, focusing only on Luke.

Claudia floated near him. 'Or you could use that electronic device of yours and defuse all the explosives. That'll solve everyone's problems.'

Hall's hand shook as he spoke. 'There's no chance of that happening. Tell him to stop, or we'll all die right now.'

There was no fear in his eyes, no lack of conviction or determination; he was ready to sacrifice us all.

'What about President Dixon, Captain?' I said. 'Who'll save him if this plane crashes?'

He turned his head slightly to me, his hand trembling as he pushed the gun closer to Luke.

'How many teams do you think we have in reserve, kid, in case something goes wrong?'

I'd been naïve not to consider it. 'A lot.'

'Damn right we have. The next one will be in the air two minutes after we hit the ground.'

I didn't doubt it. I moved my head next to the dust devil.

'It's up to you, Luke, but think of the thousands of people we're on our way to save.'

He looked at me and grinned. Then his hand stopped vibrating and he offered it to me. I shook it as the four red lights opposite blinked off.

'It's nice to meet you, Cassie.' His grip was light. 'So tell me, how did you end up in this pickle?'

A vast combined sigh of relief erupted across from me as Hall holstered his gun. He muttered under his breath and returned to his troops. I settled into my uncomfortable seat and tried to relax. Luke was next to me as Claudia continued to float.

So I answered his question.

'It's all been a big misunderstanding. These military goons just got the wrong person.'

'Ha!' Colleen spat the two letters into the air. 'That's a load of bullshit. We all know you killed the president and loads of others.' She had the cigarette packet in her hands again but must have thought better of it when she saw the scorch mark on her leg. 'How did a brat like you do that? What are you, a demon or something?'

It was Allister's turn to spray laughter through the plane. 'No, she's not one of my brethren, neither is she an angel. I don't know what she is. Maybe she's one of Olivia's Section 25 traitors sent here to spy on us.'

Claudia wagged a finger at him. 'You're an idiot. She's the ....'

I grabbed her leg before she finished the sentence. There was no need to let any of them know I was the Arcane, especially since I was powerless.

'I'm nobody, no one, nothing. You needn't worry about me.'

'Then why are you here, Cassie?' Luke said.

'It's three hours before we land,' Hall shouted down the carriage. 'So you might as well get to know each other in your monster club.' It was an excellent excuse for me to ignore the question and offer one of my own.

'Tell me, Luke, what does a dust devil do in Harlem?'

His smile was warm enough to melt an iceberg. 'I keep the streets clean.'

'And how do you do that?'

Claudia dropped on the other side of him, so he pushed up against my leg. There was a chill everywhere in the plane, but there, in that space the two of us occupied, heat spread up the whole of my body.

'I remove the Powder Gangs from their positions of power one block at a time.' He held a hand in front of me and twitched his fingers one by one. When he got to the thumb, all of his hand vibrated, and I noticed the others sitting opposite me pull close together and put their arms across their chests.

Luke must have seen it, too. 'You've nothing to worry about, my fellow Omega members.'

What he'd manipulated were the dirt particles in the plane. They lifted from the ground, off the walls and danced in the air. It was hard to see most of them in the half-light until one of the Special Ops turned on his head-light and looked in our direction. The illumination from him sliced through the gloom and highlighted how Luke controlled the surrounding dust.

Colleen snorted. 'That's a lame power.'

She opened her mouth and I thought she'd insult him

again; instead, her lips trembled and she uttered a low-pitched warble, sounding like a hummingbird. Luke's dust scattered to the four corners of the plane in a frenzy, with bits of it hitting Claudia in the head.

'Hey!' Claudia shouted as she grabbed at her face. 'Watch what you're doing.'

Luke grinned. 'It's easy to get into the drug bags and make them explode from the inside. I don't even have to be in the building to do it.'

I flicked dust from my leg. 'You're a local hero, then?'

He shrugged. 'I do my best for my community.' He glanced down at Hall and the others. 'At least, I did until these people dragged me away and threw me into the back of a van.'

Claudia slapped him on the knee. 'I used to know a Luke from Harlem.'

His blue eyes sparkled like a Caribbean sea. 'Well, it is a big place.'

'He was an ex-con turned private eye, hard as nails, with a penchant for yellow shirts. I tried to talk him into wearing better clothes, but he'd never listen to me.'

Luke and I laughed together, and it was as if I'd known him for years. He spoke more about his life, his parents and younger sister, college and working in a second-hand bookshop. All the while, Claudia serenaded us with a range of musical classics, from Marvin Gaye to Prince and any number of Motown girl groups: she had a fantastic singing voice.

When Luke finished, I told him a bit of myself – with no mention of who my mother was or the Arcane or the archangels Lucy and Michael who fought over Alice and me; only the good bits. He never mentioned my involvement in the last president's murder, but he asked about my sister.

'Do you miss Alice?'

I considered the answer as the plane lurched up and the lights flashed red at our throats.

15 ALICE: AZIZ

'I'm not sure this will work,' Bella said as I returned to the car. The gloom was fast approaching.

I wiped a bit of salad from my lips. 'What do you mean?'

She removed her cap. 'Demons are strong because they were made from Lucy's blood. They're a virus she created to infect a human host.' She opened her hand and flexed her fingers. 'If what you say is true, and that building contains a gaggle of demons and a Demon Lord, I doubt the two of us are powerful enough to overcome them.'

'You said you needed blood, and that's the only type you'll get.'

'I know, Alice.' She slapped her wrist. 'There's to be no human blood for me, but perhaps it would be better to hang around here for a few days and pick off a few demon stragglers when they leave the police station. Then I can regain my strength without putting us at risk.'

I slammed my palm against the seat and rattled the car.

'No, I'm not wasting any more time. We get this done tonight.'

'So, what's the plan? There'll be cameras everywhere and civilians inside, so there's no way of keeping what we do secret from the authorities.'

'I don't care. When they took Cassie, they declared war on her and me. What happens from now is on their heads.' The whole world could learn about the supernatural for all I cared. I just had to find my mother and sister.

'Then you should let me go in first. They don't know me. Once I drain a few of them, I'll be fighting fit.'

'I don't want you killing innocent people. That's not part of the plan.'

'So what is?'

'I'll ask for Aziz. They know me and will take me to him. After five minutes, you enter and cause havoc.'

Bella's eyes lit up. 'I can do that.'

I pointed at her. 'You only attack demons, no humans. You understand?'

She nodded. 'Then I'll search for you?'

'I'll make enough of a commotion. I shouldn't be hard to find.'

The light was vanishing as I got out of the car. I gave her one last look as I crossed the road. There was a slight hesitation as I strode up the steps and into the police station. It was a hive of activity inside, men and women talking about things I couldn't hear.

The woman on the reception desk ran her fingers over a keyboard and peered into a computer screen. I coughed loudly. She jerked her head up and glared at me through pale brown eyes. In an instant, they transformed into bright purple. I guessed she recognised me.

'Tell Aziz, Alice Arcane is here to see him.'

She sprang from her seat. Behind her, six of her

colleagues turned to me with purple rain burning in their faces.

'What?' the woman said.

I held out my arms. 'You can cuff me if it'll make you feel better.'

She picked up a phone and whispered into it. It was a brief conversation. She glanced behind her, and four of her demon associates strode towards me. I grinned at them.

'Don't worry, boys. I come in peace. Just take me to your leader.'

I moved from the desk. Two of the demons stood ahead of me, and two behind. Four of them leaving with me left three remaining, including the receptionist. That should be enough for Bella, even in her weakened condition.

I walked between them like meat in a sandwich. We left the reception and exited into a small corridor. It was narrow, so the few people there had to move as we approached. All of them appeared to be human.

We went through a door at the end and up three flights of stairs. The demons took me into a room and I knew the two waiting for me: Aziz and the woman who'd pushed me into an open grave. She'd dyed her hair red since then.

Aziz bared his teeth in an attempt at a warm greeting. 'I'm surprised to see you again, Alice Arcane, but your return has made Sasha happy.'

'We weren't formally introduced when she tried to bury my sister and me alive.'

He indicated for me to sit, but I didn't. The four demons remained in the room. I peered into Aziz's eyes and saw fear; anger possessed Sasha's face.

'Your sister is in a terrible place. Did you come here to join her?'

My heart throbbed against my ribs. 'You know where

Cassie is?' It was over five minutes since I'd entered the police station. Bella should have been inside by now.

'The Americans have her in a prison she'll never escape from. You won't see her again.' He took one step towards me. 'But I'm curious as to why you've come here. In your grief for your sister, have you given up on life?'

'You're a means to an end, Aziz. I'll admit when I walked in, I didn't care what happened to you, but now I'm looking forward to the two of you getting what you deserve.'

He stared at me before laughing. 'My dear girl, you may have escaped last time, but it won't happen again.' He rolled up his sleeves and flashed his fangs. 'You're about to die in this room.'

Sasha crept towards me as the four demons barricaded the door. Bella should have been there by now, but I heard nothing but the increased beating of my heart. I stuck out my shoulders and pushed my back into the wall, watching the demons inch nearer to me while picturing Bella abandoned in that forest so long ago. I'd been abandoned as well, or so I'd thought for most of my life. But it hadn't been like that for my mother because she'd sent Cassie and me away to save us, not to hurt us.

Now it was my turn to save them both, my mother and sister.

But I'd been betrayed again.

The wall dug into my spine as the muscles in my legs trembled.

'I'm not here to kill you, Aziz, but if you force me to, I will.'

My words were defiant, but I didn't feel it.

'We've all heard the miraculous stories about your sister, Alice Arcane, of what she did to wipe out a room of demon-possessed humans, but you're just an ordinary girl. What makes you think you can fight off my foot soldiers, never mind Sasha and me?'

The quartet of demon coppers drifted nearer to me.

'You'll find out soon enough, Demon Lord.' There was that defiance again; only it was still so many hollow words.

Then the four of them jumped towards me together.

I twisted to the side, avoiding the clawed hands reaching for my face, but I couldn't escape the one who grabbed me and threw me across the room. My legs bounced over the table, smashing into the chair, and then the far wall. Concrete met my head and pain surged through my cheek. Imaginary cartoon birds circled above me as the demons came again.

Then Aziz held up his hand and they stopped. He knelt towards me, his face so close he could have ripped my throat out.

'She's not like her sister after all.'

I wiped the blood from my lips. 'You were bluffing, then, about me?'

He shrugged. 'The reports about your twin, of what she did in America, are quite disturbing. So I couldn't take any chances with you, though it looks like my people can take their time and have some fun with you.'

Aziz stood and moved back from me, leaving space for Sasha to move forward. That's when I noticed the burn mark across her throat. She ran her fingers over it.

'Your sister did this to me in the priory, do you remember?'

I nodded. 'And now I'll finish the job.'

It was false bravado since I had no strength in me.

And the demons came for me again.

Purple eyes glared close to my face and clawed fingers reached for me.

Then the door exploded in a frenzy of violence. Wood splintered into the room as a blur of arms and teeth decapitated heads and spilt guts all over the place. When the ferocity ended, Bella stood in front of me. Demon blood slithered down her chin as she lifted Sasha into the air. With a flick of her wrist, the vampire broke the demon's neck. She tossed the body at Aziz's feet.

'Sorry I'm late, Alice.' She wiped death from her lips. 'I'd forgotten how good this tastes.'

The only thing I could taste was the mayhem in the ether. 'At least you're here now.'

Bella grinned at me, and then turned to Aziz. 'You should snack on this one. He'll really put a spark in your plug.'

It was the Demon Lord's turn to force his back into the wall. He took out his phone and showed it to us.

'There's no way out for you two. Police reinforcements are here. You can't fight all of them. And even if you try, your faces will be all over the media.'

On his mobile were dozens of flashing lights and uniformed officers pulling up outside the building.

Bella turned to me. 'I'm game if you are.'

'No. Most of those people could be innocent humans. We're not starting a slaughter here.'

My vampire partner looked around the room before laughing at me.

'I'm afraid it's too late for that, Alice.'

I snatched the device from Aziz. His fingers shook and he offered me no resistance. Dozens of officers were outside and on the screen. I pushed the phone into his face.

'You're the Demon Lord of this area. You could order them all to withdraw.'

He turned his lips up at me. 'Most of those coppers are

human. They won't leave now you and your pet vampire have transformed this into a hostage situation. This story will be trending on social media as we speak. Soon they'll be saying it's another terrorist attack and linking it to the others. There's no escape for you apart from surrendering to me.'

I was considering his words while trying to keep my breathing under control. Was it true, and were we trapped inside the police station? I examined his face and did my best to ignore our perilous position.

'Why don't you leave this body and find another?' Even in my present situation, I was curious as to how demons possessed humans. He didn't answer, but Bella did.

'There are no humans left in the building for him to possess, and the ones outside are too far away.' She laughed in his face. 'Isn't that right, My Lord?' His silence spoke volumes.

I dropped the phone at his feet and scanned every inch of the room. Then I turned to Bella and pointed to the corner.

'You can leave that way.'

She strode to my side. 'What?'

'That's a ventilation shaft.'

'And?'

'So, you turn into a bat and fly out of here, or become smoke and drift away.'

Bella grabbed her stomach and coughed laughter from her guts.

'You want me to abandon you?'

'There's no point in both of us getting caught in this demon trap. You leave, and I'll deal with this.'

Bella straightened her body and gazed into my eyes. 'You'd sacrifice yourself for me?'

She sounded as surprised as I felt. I gave her a simple one-word answer.

'Yes.'

Bella put her hand on my shoulder and pulled me close to her.

'If you give up now, you'll never rescue your mother from my brother. You'll never see your sister again. She'll rot in an American prison for the rest of her life. Is that what you want?'

A runaway train sped through my guts and my head was ready to explode.

'We have no other choice.'

'We do. You have the option I gave you at the Nexus.' She spun me around so I faced the Demon Lord. 'Drink his blood and you'll have some of your abilities again. You'll be able to teleport both of us out of here. And then we'll find my brother and your mother. We'll rescue your sister after that.'

Bella's energy flowed through her fingers and into me. What she'd said was true, but I couldn't do it.

'You said demon blood could kill me.'

She let go of me and screamed. Her anguish hurt my ears.

'What risks are you prepared to take to see your family again?' Bella pushed me against the wall. 'You want me to leave so you can abandon Cassie. Is that it?'

My body shook in her grip. My flesh was weak and my mind shrank under the pressure. Was this how my life would end? I stared at her, and then at Aziz: a demon who'd tried to kill me twice. We'd come here so Bella could drink demon blood to regain her strength and the connection with her brother.

So why couldn't I take a risk as well?

Was I ready to abandon Cassie and my mother?

Of course not.

I turned to Bella. 'I'll do it.'

Bella's reply was instant, slitting the Demon Lord's throat with one flick of her fingers. Her mouth snapped at his neck as his true form tried to leave the body, purple mist seeping from his eyes, but going nowhere as he slid down the wall.

Then she lifted him.

'Now, we both drink from this, Alice.'

I joined her at Aziz's neck. His blood was warm and sweet as I drank like a thirsty woman in the desert. The blood flowed into me and I felt magnificent. I was addicted and thrust my head into his flesh.

'This is intoxicating.'

She tried to pull me away as Aziz struggled in my grasp.

'That's enough, Alice.' Her hand was in mine, but I couldn't stop, my bloodied face buried in his neck. 'Stop, Alice.' The room stank of death. 'It's time for you to teleport us to the car. Can you do that?'

I lifted from Aziz, twisting my head to stare at her, and then at the camera flickering red above. Peering straight into the lens, I was reluctant to remove the demon blood glistening on my lips. I stared at the body of the Demon Lord and felt capable of anything. I squeezed Bella's hand and we disappeared from the room.

16 CASSIE: BONDING

The red flickered for thirty seconds and the heat spread through my neck as I clawed at it. Electricity shimmered under my skin and I felt a pulse against my flesh. The air smelt of burning metal as I gazed into Claudia's eyes and thought of Alice. Claudia took my hand as I reached into my brain for an Arcane trigger, searching for the power to neutralise the bomb humming inside me.

The plane bounced up as if someone had hold of the wings and was shaking it from side to side.

Then the lights went off on everyone's necks, but my heart kept thumping. I looked down at Hall: he had the electronic trigger in his hand as he grinned at me before he slipped it into his pocket. Omega Team breathed a collective sigh of relief.

Was it an accident caused by the turbulence, or had he done it on purpose to remind us who was in charge? I was considering those things when Luke asked me the question again.

'Do you miss Alice?'

I rubbed at the missing part of my ear and gave him an honest answer.

'I miss her every minute of the day, but I try not to dwell on it; otherwise, I'd be too miserable to work out how I'll get out of this mess.'

'Do you believe we can survive this?'

'I've always been a glass half full girl, Luke, no matter how crappy the situation.'

As I kept on convincing myself of this, I noticed the shaman staring at me. So I stared back.

'Tell me, Sayan, shouldn't a female shaman be called a shawoman?'

When her eyes glittered, it was as if all the knowledge of the universe was inside those pale green pupils.

'The technical term is shamanka.'

She was a woman of few words. So I continued.

'Is it true a shamanka interacts with the spirit world?' In the time I'd been dabbling with the supernatural, I'd met many creatures, from archangels to demons, including the Devil, and had even travelled to Limbo, Purgatory and Hell, but I'd never seen a ghost.

Sayan sat there in silence. I was thinking of something else to say when Claudia spoke.

'I dated a poltergeist once, but it didn't work out.'

My eyebrows twitched. 'What happened?'

'Well, I was living in France at the time, and this girl, this poltergeist, was killed during the Revolution, so she had loads of great gossip about Danton, Robespierre and Marat, but she left so much mess in the house, it drove me crazy. And the constant banging on the walls and moving the furniture everywhere did my head in. So I moved to Berlin and shacked up with Louise Brooks for a while.'

'How old are you?' Luke asked her.

Claudia scratched her nose. 'Sixteen on my last birth-day, but that was - oh let me see - about two hundred years ago.'

Sayan pointed at Claudia. 'All those who have died are around you.'

My friend laughed. 'It's going to get pretty cramped in here, then.'

'They are the spirits of those you've killed, vampire.' Sayan had a voice dragged up from some deep, dark abyss. Then she changed her focus to Captain Hall and the Special Ops. 'I see the dead yet to be surrounding those in uniform.' The demon was next on her list. 'Blood flows over this one like all the oceans combined to cover the world.' Then the banshee. 'Multitudes of spirits scream and scream because of her.' And then she peered at me, but there was only silence.

I folded my arms and pondered how much rest I should get before we landed.

'Don't keep me in suspense, Sayan.' I rubbed my damaged ear. 'I'm tougher than I look.'

She removed her seatbelt and stood. At the other end of the carriage, I noticed Hall getting twitchy again. We were hours away from the Zone, and he was already a bag of nerves. Sayan stepped next to me, twisting her head to gaze into my face. Her long, dark locks appeared to twitch like ripples on top of a lake, the green of her eyes transforming into a thousand tiny glittering stars.

'You are empty, child.' An aroma of summer flowers drifted from her hair, which rippled to the point I thought she might use it to strangle me.

'Well, I've never claimed to have the most sparkling of personalities. I think my sister got that.'

Alice. Where was she? As much as I was glad she wasn't on this plane and travelling to certain death with us, I also wished she was with me. She would have loved to meet all these unique supernatural people. But was that the correct term for them, or even for me?

Sayan reached out and touched my cheek; her fingers were warm and soft as she moved across my face and under my nose. Then she went to the missing part of my ear.

'You're a young girl who has lived more than you let on. For most of your life, you were lost and alone, isolated when surrounded by others. But all that changed when you met her; reunited with your other half.'

She pulled from me, but I grabbed her arm.

'What do you know about Alice?'

Everyone on the plane focused on us. I imagined those dust particles circling me, waiting for Colleen to fire them across the carriage with her deathly tones.

'Who the fuck is Alice?' the demon said.

'I see nothing around you but her,' Sayan said. 'You have no past, no present, and no future, Cassandra Kane; not without her.' She returned to her seat. 'But there is one other; one other who will decide your fate, for good or bad.'

'Is that my mother? Do you mean Mary?'

Sayan strapped herself in again. 'All I see is a shadow of the one; I'm unsure whether you should embrace them or flee.'

The silence cut through the air, so the only noise above the engines was the beating of my heart. Then there was a loud bang as the demon clapped his hands.

'Well, this is much better than Travel Scrabble or Monopoly to keep us occupied on the journey. Unless anyone has a pack of cards. I haven't played poker for ages.'

He scrutinised me. 'Though I'm not sure what we could play for.'

I returned his scrutiny. 'Tell me about Pandora.'

He turned his nose up at me. 'I said everything back at that prison; there's nothing else to say.'

'Do you understand how I know you're lying, Allister? Because your lips are moving.'

'Why do you think he's lying, Cassie?' Luke said.

'All demons lie; they can't help themselves because it's in their nature. This is why the Devil loves them so much.'

Allister waved his hand at me. 'Poppycock and nonsense. I've never even met the Queen of Lies. Lucy doesn't waste her time with lesser demons like me.'

'If you're such a lesser demon, how come you know so much about what we're heading towards? What is it about Pandora you're not telling us?'

'And what will you do if I don't tell you?'

'Me? I'll do nothing. But I'll get Luke to force all the dust in this plane down your throat and fill your lungs with it.' Without me asking, Luke held out his hand and it shimmered. The demon's pupils turned a nightmarish shade of purple. 'What happens to you when your human host dies, Allister? What becomes of your true self when there's nobody to possess?' He didn't reply, only staring at Luke as the dust devil created a swirling ball of dirt between us and the demon. 'It's okay; you needn't tell me. I've killed enough demons to know what happens when the possession comes to a violent end: you return to your original form, a purple cloud searching for another human meatsack to live inside.' We all glanced down at Captain Grant and his troops. 'I've seen the results when you don't find a host in time, and it isn't pretty.' His eyes were nothing but purple now.

Colleen flicked at the lighter in her hand. 'What happens to a demon?'

'They swirl around like a trapped fly trying to get out of a room, banging up against walls and solid objects. Then, when they can't find a live human, they pull apart and split into nothing. I assume it's excruciating.' I smiled at him. 'At least, I hope it is.'

He tried to grin, but it wasn't right, with half of his face looking as if he'd had a stroke. 'I'll be down inside one of those grunts before anyone can stop me.'

I shook my head. 'I think you're lying again, Allister. If it's that easy for you to find a new host, why are you trapped in that body? The bomb in your neck shouldn't scare you. Why would it when you can leave at any time?' I glanced down to Hall. 'What is it that Section 25 has over you if it's not the explosive?'

'You'll never know, child.' The sparkle had returned to his grin.

Claudia floated again as she spoke. 'According to legend, Zeus created Pandora as a punishment for man after Prometheus stole fire from Heaven and gave it to mortals. She was the first woman and was given a jar containing all manner of misery and evil, which she let loose upon the world because of her curiosity.'

'I thought it was a box she had?' I tried to remember my history lessons from the few times I went to school.

'No, that was a 16th-century mistranslation by the Dutch humanist Desiderius Erasmus.' Claudia looked at me. 'Maybe our Doctor Olivia is related to him. Anyway, can you imagine creating a tale where women are blamed for all the evils in this world?' She glanced at the humans hanging on her every floating word. 'And Zeus was always changing himself into swans and horses and all kinds of things just to have sex. How deranged is that?' The demon must have thought we'd forgotten about him, but Claudia hadn't. 'Explain what this Pandora has to do with the legend.'

Six of the Omega Team turned on him, our eyes peering deep into his demon gaze; there was no escape for him on this flight of ours into a blue Hell. I think he was about to refuse again when Luke flicked his wrist and a ball of spinning dust flew at the demon's head. He threw up his arms in defence, but Luke stopped it a few inches from Allister's face. Then he lowered his hands and spoke.

'Like most myths and legends, what you said is half truth and half fiction. It wasn't Zeus who created Pandora, but a cabal of fallen angels. Those God cast out of Heaven after the First of the Fallen; those that desired human women and went against all of God's demands.'

My heartbeat doubled in speed. 'Those fallen angels became the fathers of the Nephilim, the children born from the union of angels and human women.'

And the last of the Nephilim is my mother.

'Yes, but God sent the Great Flood to destroy all the Nephilim. A few of the fallen angels still lived and they formed a plan to create the perfect woman for them.'

I clutched at my chest. 'I think I'm going to be sick.'

Colleen burst out laughing. 'I don't know why people are surprised when they discover that most of the world's religions were created to enslave women, in one form or another. They tell lies, making a woman responsible for all the ills in the world, or they say women are inferior to men because they came from a man's rib, or they proclaim women as being good for nothing but spitting out babies and keeping the home clean.' She had a cigarette in her hand, but she didn't light it, only rolling it between her fingers.

'You should have seen what it was like for me growing up in Ireland, where I was the only girl in a house with four brothers and a father who thought it was the 1950s.' She crushed the poison stick and dropped the damage to the floor.

The pain in my chest diminished a little as I focused on the demon.

'So you're saying a group of fallen angels, who fathered the Nephilim, created Pandora as their, as their...' I couldn't finish the words.

'She was to be their communal wife.'

Claudia sat next to me. 'Now I understand why she wants to come back and eat the world.'

The sickness returned to me, but I needed to know more.

'How did they create her? Did they give her the powers she's using in Valhalla?'

Allister shrugged. 'What I'm telling you is what has been passed down through demon lore for centuries, over two thousand years at least.'

'And how do we stop her?' That was all that mattered.

'That part of the legend has been lost to time. All I know is a group of warlocks and wizards, witches and mystics banished her to another realm. How she's returned is anyone's guess.' And with that, he sat back and crossed his arms.

I thought of Pandora coming from the angels who'd created the Nephilim and its similarity to my lineage. Perhaps we were second cousins, thousands of years removed. It was Captain Hall's voice that broke me from those thoughts.

'We'll be landing in ten minutes. When we get off, head to the large tent in front of you. We have five minutes to go over the plan, and then we move into the Zone.'

I held on to Claudia as the plane descended, all the time wondering if I could kill a woman who'd been wronged so much.

17 ALICE: LONDON

We reappeared outside. Mist swirled around my head while my guts tried to punch their way through my ribs. A vision of Aziz shimmered in front of me as the taste of demon blood clung to my lips. A craving deep inside me refused to go away as the ghostly Demon Lord reached for me and grinned. I grasped for his shining purple fingers and missed.

I fell into the side of the car. My head hit the glass as I spewed all over the ground. Thousands of tiny drummers beat their way through my limbs and settled on thrashing my brain into submission. I was heading for Newcastle concrete when Bella pulled me up.

'Give me the keys, Alice.'

Daggers jabbed at my fingers as I fumbled in my pocket and gave her them. Liquid lead flowed through my legs and threatened to drag me underground. Only Bella's grip kept me upright.

'Can you drive?' My voice sounded strange to me, like a radio station struggling to stay in tune.

Bella took the keys and opened the door. 'These modern cars are new to me, but I observed you on the way here, and I'm a quick learner.' She dragged me into the back. I flopped there and dreamt of dying. Bella climbed into the driver's seat and leant over to stare at me wallowing in confusion and agony.

I grabbed my stomach in a failed attempt at squeezing the pain from me.

'What's happening to me?' It hadn't been this bad when I'd teleported before or used my other Arcane abilities.

'The Demon Lord's blood is very rich, like champagne bubbles for a first-time drinker.' Her grin only made me feel worse. 'Your body will adjust to it, eventually.'

I twisted to the side and threw up again. 'How long will it take?' The car stank, but the fire rushing through my veins distracted me from the aroma.

'You should be okay when we get to London.'

'London's about three hundred miles away.' I managed to spit the words out. 'I won't be better until then?'

'Don't worry,' she said. 'If the pain gets too much, you'll probably black out.'

The car pulled off and I rolled on to my hip to escape the stench. I pushed my face into the leather, my chest fighting to split through my ribs. Water filled my eyes as my vision faded and Bella drove from the mayhem.

Police lights and sirens possessed my senses as I wriggled further into the back seat. The taste of the Demon Lord stuck to my throat like dead flies in a spider's web. I wanted to sleep, but all that came to me was Aziz's face as I drank his existence away. His eyes became mine as every terrible thing he'd ever done, each life he'd taken, flashed before me. Throats were ripped out, hearts torn from bodies, limbs flailing as they were lashed and cut from terrified victims.

Each of his horrific actions sped across my skull, wails of pain pushing me deep into the car. His fingers brought death, and it kept on going, falling further and further back through the years, the veil of time tumbling from his eyes and mine until I found my aching bones gazing into shimmering bright light.

A sound shrieked through my ears, vibrated out of my head and down my spine. I was inside someone else's flesh, legs trembling as my knees bent and I stared at a howling, disappointed whirlwind. A heavenly illumination lifted the body that wasn't mine, tossing me into the ether so I spiralled through the clouds and the wind.

I went down and down, falling and falling, and the only thing surpassing my pain was anger and frustration at my treatment. The descent continued for an eternity until I hit the ground with a thump. My shoulder rippled in agony as I rolled to the side and gripped my stomach. An electric sea of suffering bellowed through me in endless waves. Death was all I required, but it never came.

Eventually, sleep found me.

I WOKE up sometime later and crawled to the window. We were parked in some country lane, with overhanging trees draped against the windscreen. Bella was not in the front seat. Electricity seeped through my legs as I pushed up. My face was pressed into the glass, my skull banging like fireworks exploding on New Year's Eve.

Aziz had disappeared from inside my head, and all I

could see were glimpses of Cassie and my mother. They spoke to me with soundless words, their lips moving, but nothing coming out. They stood together, arms outstretched towards me before an invisible force snatched them away and they vanished into my memories.

I slithered from the window and wanted to die again. Something hit the car as I struggled to stay awake. Red eyes melted against the glass as I peered into them. My hand was on my throat as Bella grinned at me and I sank into an abyss of sleep.

MY MIND DRIFTED in and out of nightmares before I woke once more. I lifted my head out of bed and stared at a wall covered in exotic paintings. Old men with distinguished faces gazed at me.

'I hated the decor in this place when I bought it in the 1930s.' Bella stood over me with a glass of juice. It smelt of bananas.

My arms and legs throbbed as I sat up. 'What happened to me?'

My vampire partner screwed her lips and narrowed her eyes. 'You took a big sleep while I brought you here.'

I pulled the sheets up to my chin and glanced at my aching limbs. 'Why am I naked?'

Bella sat on the bed and smiled at me. 'No sensible person sleeps with clothes on unless you're in the middle of winter or the Antarctic.' She stood. 'Plus, I have to say, your garments smelled worse than a whorehouse in the plague. I washed them while you slept the sleep of the innocent.' She turned her lips up at me. 'There's no need to thank me, Alice Arcane.'

'How did we get here?'

Bella held her hands in the air. 'When you teleported us from the police station, I combined my memories of driving from the 1940s with my observations of you motoring from Lindisfarne to Newcastle and concocted the perfect road journey to here.' She sucked at one side of her cheek. 'There were only a few accidents along the way, but I don't think anyone noticed. But you have reminded me to dispose of the body in the boot.'

I ignored the glint in her eye and assumed she was joking. 'And where is here?'

She joined me on the bed once more.

'We're in Soho. I bought this place in the 1930s, and one of my faithful adherents and their descendants have kept it going ever since.' She took my hand. 'You wouldn't believe what it's worth now compared to what I paid for it.'

'We escaped from Newcastle?'

'Not only that, but the authorities covered up the truth of what happened, though they are turning it into an attack against the country.'

I pulled the sheets closer to me, feeling more vulnerable than I had for a long time.

'What do you mean?'

'The government, using the media, is twisting our activities with the Demon Lord in Newcastle and connecting it with your earlier assault against the prime minister. They're not naming names, but they're linking it to a larger terrorist attack on the nation. There's no mention of the supernatural, of course, not yet, but I don't think it will be long before the inhuman cat is out of the bag. Meanwhile, they've upgraded the State of Emergency, with increased military patrols, and our job's got even harder.' She beamed at me. 'But apart from that, are you feeling better?'

My back sank into the bed. 'A shower and something to eat might brighten me up.'

'Great.' Bella stood. 'Your clothes are clean and in the corner. The bathroom is to the right. I'll go downstairs and use the kitchen, which has been idle for more than eighty years. When you smell the burning toast, you'll know it's time to come down.'

She swept out of the room before I could reply. I crawled from the bed, legs struggling as my toes sank into the carpet. I stumbled into the bathroom and grabbed the sink; a tired reflection stared at me from the mirror. My face was pale and ready to drop. Inside those eyes, all I saw was Cassie and the disappointment of letting her down. Was this how I'd rescue her from that American imprisonment?

I turned from the other me and stepped into the shower. Once I'd switched it on, I stood under the hot water for five minutes and hoped it would wash away my guilt. It didn't. Then I dried off and got dressed. I followed the smell of cooked food into the kitchen. Bella was munching on a burnt sausage as I entered.

'I thought vampires couldn't eat human food.'

She pulled something from between her teeth. 'We can eat whatever we want, but it means nothing. It's like listening to heavy metal music. It's a distraction which is ultimately pointless.' Her grin unnerved me. 'And anyway, who's saying this is human food in the way you mean?'

I sat down and scooped up a forkful of scrambled eggs.

'You drove from Newcastle into London and this place where you haven't lived since the 1940s?'

'Aren't you glad we're partners?'

'Why did we come here?' The eggs slipped down my throat as I picked up a slice of burnt bread.

Bella finished the sausage and I tried not to watch her eat it. 'While the demon blood allowed you to teleport us to safety from that police station and also made you sick, it brought me back to full health and reconnected me to my dear brother.'

I dropped the toast into the eggs. 'You know where Dracula is?'

She grinned. 'I'm aware he's in London. It will take me a little while to narrow down his precise spot.'

I picked up the glass of orange juice and drank it in one go.

'For once, I think things are going my way.'

Bella rose from the table. 'Have your breakfast and regain your strength. Then we should be ready to make our next move.' She made to leave before turning to me. 'What's it feel like with the demon blood coursing through your veins?'

The taste of orange juice in my mouth turned to acid. I grasped at my throat and fought off the desire to throw up.

'I think it's gone from me now. I don't feel any different.'

Bella's smile was bright enough to light up the night. 'You can lie to yourself, Alice, but it's a waste of time doing it to me. You should admit what it was like supping on the Demon Lord's blood.'

I wiped a piece of the egg from my lips. 'I did what I had to do to get us out of there, and it nearly killed me. I thought I was going to die outside the police station.' I got up from the table and pushed the chair backwards in a mock show of anger. 'That was a one-time thing. I won't be doing it again.'

'So, there'll be no more angel or demon blood for you?'

I glared at her. 'That's what I said.'

Bella waved her hand in the air. 'Then let's see what you're willing to do when the lives of your sister and mother are on the line.'

She left the kitchen and I stood there, transfixed.

I knew exactly what the answer would be to her words.

18 CASSIE: THE TENT

The plane landed with a bump. Claudia, even with her claim of perfect balance, whacked her head on the roof. She rubbed her forehead as everyone unstrapped and prepared for what waited outside.

I glanced at the others, watching the troops checking their weapons while Hall whispered into the communicator near his face. Claudia licked the blood from her fingers and grinned at me. Luke mumbled something under his breath while Colleen fiddled with an unlit cigarette. Allister glared at me as the rest of the supernatural team sat there in silence. Then Hall barked at everyone.

'Everybody out, now.'

Nobody argued. We stepped off the plane and into a field. I saw no living thing there, heard no birds in the air, but there was the aroma of something unpleasant lingering everywhere.

'What is that stink?' I said.

Claudia pushed up against me. 'Isn't it obvious, Cassie?' Her nose twitched like that witch from an old TV show. 'That's the sweet smell of death waiting for us.'

We moved through the field and headed for the large tent ahead. As I was about to step in, I glanced to my right and froze at the sight: in the distance, but getting closer, a blue cloud swept across the horizon so there was no more green. The silence was deafening, no sounds of nature, and the only thing in the air was the Zone consuming everything in its path. Beneath that was an ancient being we were supposed to prevent from swallowing up another town, then this country, and probably the world.

And somewhere deep down inside of me, all I could think about was if Alice and my mother were safe.

Then, the enormity of what we were about to do hit me full in the chest, and my heart trembled as if plugged into an electric socket. Still, I'd stopped a nuclear Armageddon only a week ago, so how difficult would this be?

I turned from the cloud covering the horizon, but a sliver of blue continued to blur my vision. Captain Hall spoke to Erasmus on the phone as I strode into the tent. The Special Ops waited on orders while the rest of us just waited.

Claudia stood next to me.

'Killing a president is much more exciting than saving one, don't you think?'

I didn't reply and checked our surroundings instead: half a dozen scientists were packing up to leave, heading out to the plane. Hall finished his call and spoke to the commander of the post. It was a brief, animated conversation, and the other man looked relieved when it was over. When he left, there were only thirteen of us remaining.

I pushed my face close to Claudia. 'When we're inside this mist, make sure we don't get separated, no matter what they want us to do.'

Claudia ran her fingers across her throat. 'What are we going to do about these?'

It was an important question, but I had no answer to it.

'We'll have to play it by ear, but let's look for an opportunity to get the trigger from Hall.'

Claudia nodded while smiling at the others. 'What about the one Erasmus has?'

I'd thought about that during the plane journey. 'I'm hoping it's too far away to work, even though she seemed convinced it would.'

'She might have been bluffing.'

I shook my head. 'I haven't known Doctor Olivia Erasmus for long, but I don't think she's the bluffing type. Maybe, just maybe, whatever that blue cloud is, it will disrupt the signal between her trigger and the detonators in our necks. But we'll still have to get the one from Hall.'

As I whispered to Claudia, the Captain checked a map on his phone.

'The Zone will be over us in ten minutes, and then, at its current rate of speed, it'll cover the town of Barnesville an hour after that. We'll move to the truck once we've rechecked the plan.' He looked beyond me. 'Now, listen up; this is the last time we go over this before the Zone engulfs us.'

So we went over it again.

Once inside the Zone, we'd drive into the centre and head for President Dixon's family home. Someone suggested we fly there, but all the other aircraft entering the Zone had lost power within a minute. Yet the Special Ops were guessing motor vehicles would be fine. When we'd left the truck, Luke would use his ability to force the cloud from us to create a vacuum away from the blue. When he was doing that, it would be the only thing he could focus on, so he'd be extra vulnerable to attacks: it would be up to the Special Ops, plus Allister and Claudia, to protect him at all times. Colleen and I would be security and defence as we pushed into the town. Then it was up to Sayan and Wovoka to determine the best spot for the Ghost Dance, to find and communicate with the spirits of those who'd banished Pandora thousands of years ago.

And if we encountered Pandora?

Then that was down to me. And I had no special abilities.

So I asked Hall for the sixth time, 'What makes you think I can stop her?'

'Everyone has seen what you did in the presidential bunker. Teleportation, flight, invisibility and telekinesis; you possess all these. You're the strongest person on this planet, so who else would we get to face this challenge?'

And he didn't even know about the telepathy. Not that it mattered since I had none of those anymore. As much as I hated Lucy, I wished she was with us in that tent.

Was I putting everyone at risk by not telling them about my lack of special abilities? I was still strong and quick, more so than a normal human sixteen-year-old girl, but was that going to be sufficient to overpower Pandora? And was Pandora inside the Zone already, or was she still spreading her blue tentacles into our world until she was powerful enough to cross between dimensions?

The stink of smoke drifted over, and I turned to see Colleen and Allister sharing a ciggy. The demon's eyes burnt purple as he blew smoke towards me and then addressed the whole of the tent.

'Why don't we send the spirit talkers into the blue and let them find out how to defeat Pandora? Then the rest of us can go in. Trust me; it's never good to have all your apples in the same basket when your enemy is desperate to make cider.'

Hall was having none of it. 'The plan is set, demon. Get ready, or your head will be off your shoulders before we leave here.'

I still didn't get it; the demon could possess Hall or his troops or any of those who had just left. Why would he be worried about dying? I scrutinised him and the captain and considered the answer to this mystery.

And then I had a eureka moment.

I marched up to Hall. 'You have something which prevents you, stops all of you who work for Section 25, from being possessed by demons. Isn't that right?'

He grinned at me. 'I guess you're not as dumb as you look, girl.' He unbuttoned his shirt and rolled up a sleeve. 'Part of this is down to you and what you did in that bunker.' Hall showed me his wrist, but I saw nothing different with it. I glanced at the clock on the table; we had four minutes to get into the truck.

'What do you mean?'

'I'm not going to tell you how we did it, but once your killing spree led to the discovery of how many of our people were possessed, we had to stop it from happening again.' He nodded to his troops as they went to a stack of boxes in the corner. I watched them remove a pile of hazmat suits as Hall continued. 'Once the seriousness of the situation was clear, that the highest leadership positions in the world were compromised, then every government on the planet worked in unison to ensure it wouldn't happen again. Information regarding demons and the supernatural, secreted away for hundreds of years, was shared between all. And because of that, it didn't take long to come up with a solution. Your murderous actions brought governments together, girl.' He winked at me. 'You should be proud of yourself.'

I assumed whatever he was talking about was below his skin, but I couldn't see it and he wouldn't expand any further. He joined his troops and climbed into the last hazmat suit as the others zipped up. The other non-humans seemed as surprised as me by the turn of events.

'What is this, Hall?' Allister said.

'The blue mist infects by touch on the human body, but our Intel tells us it's harmless to supernaturals.'

'Are you sure about this?' I said.

Hall's grin grew wider. 'Not a hundred per cent, no.' He covered his head and zipped up. The next time I heard his voice was through the device in my ear. 'We've got two minutes to get into the truck, so let's move.'

He led his troops past us and out of the tent. The others followed, but Claudia and I stayed behind.

'If that blue gunk doesn't hurt us, then why don't we sit here and wait until they all get slaughtered, Cassie?'

The flickering red light at both of our throats was answer enough. As we stepped outside, the Zone was only a few hundred feet away and approaching rapidly. We climbed into the back of the truck. Inside, as well as the thirteen of us, was a collection of automatic rifles and ammunition. Claudia reached out and touched one.

'Oh, toys; can I have one to play with?'

Hall pointed a pistol at her. 'No.' It was a sharp single-word reply.

She scowled at him and turned to me. 'It's always the same: the boys never let the girls have any of the fun.'

Claudia wasn't treating this seriously, but I knew it was her way of staying in control of her emotions. I squashed against her in the rear, ten of us there, with the other three in the front. She stared at her nails, and I wondered if, even though she'd lived for over two centuries, she was still only a sixteen-year-old girl at heart. My mind returned to the thoughts she'd accidentally shared with me when I'd seen her memories in that presidential mansion. She'd done it so I could see where to teleport inside the bunker, to share her recollections of that place with me, to ensure I didn't reappear inside a solid object.

And that had worked. But an unfortunate side effect was my mind tumbling into the dark corners of her past, seeing how she'd suffered in that house, not only recently, but when she was younger, before she became a vampire. Her terrible history continued to stay with me, and as much as I felt like an intruder in her life, I knew it was essential to understand what she'd gone through.

A month ago, I'd believed all supernatural creatures, and especially vampires, were monsters to be killed without mercy; but now, I knew different. Looking at the rest of the Omega Team as we waited for the blue mist to swallow us up, I'd only willingly kill the demon. Colleen was strange and angry, but, from what she'd hinted at earlier, I think that was likely as much down to her family upbringing as anything else. Luke was a hero to his community, with as warm and generous a heart as anyone I'd ever met, while Wovoka and Sayan were no different from any spiritual human, except they could communicate with the dead. Now we had to hope they'd find those who'd defeated Pandora millennia ago, and we could do it again; because if everyone was relying on me to do it, then we were in big trouble.

That's all I was thinking about as the mist covered the truck and everything went blue.

19 ALICE: UNDERGROUND

The smell of burnt bread hung in the air. I picked up the last piece of toast and left. The kitchen led into the living room, where I found Bella sitting at a coffee table pouring two cups of mint tea. A tray of chocolate biscuits was on her right.

'This place looks modern considering you haven't visited since 1940.'

A large flat-screen TV covered most of the main wall. The carpet was plush and luxurious and warmed my bare feet; the furniture was a three-piece suite, three full bookcases, lights, and that coffee table.

Bella picked up a cup and sipped at it. 'The descendants of my loyal follower have lived here since I left, awaiting my return and keeping the place clean and up to date.'

I ran my fingers over the window; everywhere was dust-free.

'They just let you walk straight back in?'

She snapped a biscuit in two and allowed parts of it to crumble into the carpet.

'Once they got over the shock and picked themselves up.'

'And where are they now?'

'I gave them a few days off, a scant reward for all their years of service.'

I strode around the room, glancing at the books on the shelves and the starkness of the walls.

'Where has the money come from for all of this?'

Bella crunched through chocolate, her perfect white teeth turning a darker colour.

'Long-term monetary investments are easy for immortals. You'd be surprised at how many supernatural creatures run banks and financial institutions.'

I took the sofa opposite her and bit into a biscuit. The sugar rush made my blood pump.

'Do you know where your brother is?'

'The closer we got to London, the more aware I became of his presence. But we have a problem.'

'What problem?'

She leant down to her feet, picked up a glossy magazine and handed it to me. A clutch of Royals peered out from the front cover.

'That's our problem.'

'*Hello* magazine?'

'Read the headline.'

I dropped it onto the table and did what she said.

'It's the largest gathering of European Royals in one place since before the First World War.' I looked at her. 'What's this got to do with us?'

Bella finished her tea. 'Look inside and see the profiles of some of those attending.'

I sighed loudly as I flicked through it. Beautiful photos of vacuous people beamed out. The British Royal Family were prominent before half-page features led into small snippets of other European royalty. After a dozen pages of boredom, I gave up and glared at Bella.

'Are you trying to wind me up?'

She snatched the magazine from my hands and turned to the back. She folded it in half and pushed it into my face.

'This is our problem.'

I read the article with startled eyes. 'The last surviving member of Dracula's family will also be in attendance.'

'Quite.' She crossed her arms. 'The last surviving member, indeed.'

'What is this, Bella?'

'It's not the last surviving member of my family, but my brother, but they don't know that.' She tapped one finger against her knee. 'Or about me.'

'But why is he at a gathering for the British Royal Family?' The thought of it made my head hurt.

'The British Royal Family are related to Vlad the Impaler.'

I didn't know whether to laugh or cry.

'But they're not related to you?'

'We had different mothers. Vlad the Monk, Dracula's brother and my younger half-brother, is a direct ancestor of the British Royal Family, through a Wurttemberg princess, Mary of Teck; and she was a grandmother to Queen Elizabeth II.'

The biscuit broke between my fingers and crumbs drifted to the carpet.

'But what's he doing with them now?'

'I don't know, but I believe he's aware you're coming for him, so he's shielded himself inside Buckingham Palace. And he'll have your mother with him.'

The biscuit crumbled into a dozen pieces as I crushed it in my hand.

'How do we get past the security and inside the Palace?'

'I can think of only one way.'

Only then did I notice a glint in Bella's pupils that wasn't there at the Nexus.

'You've fed again.'

She wiped chocolate from her lips. 'Well, these biscuits are divine.'

My nostrils flared like an agitated horse's. 'You know what I mean. You drank human blood while I slept.'

Her eyes sparkled. 'I have to admit, I had a nightcap when I put you to bed.' She leant into me. 'You should try it, Alice.' She turned her nose up. 'It's so much better than that demon moonshine.'

My legs ached as I stood. 'The people who were here, the descendants of your servant, you took blood from them?'

Bella settled into the sofa. 'They offered it to me willingly. It was a great honour for them.'

'Did you kill them?'

She laughed and shook her head. 'Now, why would I do that? What a waste it would be. I bet it's hard getting good servants in this plastic age.'

Bits of chocolate stuck to my leg. I brushed them off without taking my eyes from her.

'You want me to drink more demon blood, don't you, so I can teleport us into Buckingham Palace?'

The memory of Aziz's blood, the taste of it in my mouth, clawed at my guts. I spat bits of biscuit to the floor and glared at her.

'It's the only way we can get past all the security at the Palace, Alice. Unless...'

I wiped my hand across my face. 'Unless what?'

Bella reached into her pocket and removed the coded paper. She laid it on the table so the signs peered at me.

'I haven't told you the complete truth about this.'

'Why am I not surprised?'

She pointed towards the first line of symbols. 'Do you remember when you said you'd decoded some of this?'

'It impressed Dr Rivers.'

'And me as well. But you weren't quite right. You said one of the decoded words was the Forthcoming, but you were slightly off. The correct translation is The Forge is coming.'

'The Forge?' Confusion must have rippled through my face. 'Was this Nazi creation a metal worker?'

'That was the name the Nazis gave to their supernatural super-soldier. It was a shapeshifter greater than all shapeshifters.'

'Greater in what way?'

'The information the British spies in Germany relayed to Churchill was that this shapeshifter, the Forge, was heading here to kill him and steal his identity. Not only that, but because of the Nazi experiments which created the creature, the Forge could temporarily change anyone's face. It meant the Nazis, once they replaced Churchill, could get any of their agents into the British government and the war office.'

The gravity of her words rippled through my skull. 'If this shapeshifter is still alive, they could get us inside Buckingham Palace.'

'It's our only choice if you refuse to drink the demon blood again.'

Then it was no choice at all. I scooped the coded paper off the table and offered it to her.

'There's no time like the present.'

'I don't need that anymore. That night in Balham Tube station, when everything went to pot and the Nazis killed me by proxy, I was heading to the creature's underground lair. It could still be there; it might not be, but at least it's a starting point.' She pointed towards the window. 'And it's dark outside.'

Energy and anticipation flowed through me. 'Let's go.'

'Are you sure you don't want some demon blood before we leave?' She removed a phial of red liquid from her pocket.

'You took that from Aziz?' The hairs on my arms shivered against my clothes.

'It's always good to have an emergency supply.' She wiggled it at my face. 'Yes?'

'No.' I pushed past her towards an exit I was unsure of.

Bella put her hand on my shoulder and pulled me into her.

'I have to say, Alice Arcane, being with you is the most fun I've had in a very long time.' She took me to the door and out of the property. 'Then again, I was pinned to a wall for over eighty years.' She locked up and we stepped into the street. 'And Soho is so glittery nowadays.'

My first visit to London and I'd slept all the way there. And then I remembered I was a wanted fugitive and grabbed Bella's arm.

'The police are after me.'

Her laugh was quiet enough to drift away on the evening breeze whispering around us.

'I guess they're after many in this city. But don't worry, I thought of everything.' She reached into her pocket, removed a scrunched baseball cap and handed it to me. 'Put this on and you'll be fine.'

I did as instructed and walked with her. People filled

the streets as we marched past shops, bars, and restaurants. There was a gorgeous-smelling veggie place on the way, and I nearly stumbled towards it thanks to the pull of the aromas seeping through its open windows. A memory crawled up from my stomach and into my throat as I tasted Aziz's demon blood and wanted to gag. I focused on Bella as a distraction.

'How do you know the way to the Tube station after all these years away?'

She talked as we walked, reaching into a vivid red leather jacket which made me realise she'd changed clothes since Newcastle.

'The guardian of my property gave me this.' She had an expensive-looking mobile phone in her hand. 'I've had a lovely time exploring it while you napped.' Bella held the screen towards me. 'We get on at Piccadilly Circus Station and off at Balham. It should only take about twenty-five minutes.' She weaved her arm through mine. 'We can spend that time getting to know each other.'

Bella scanned our surroundings as we went while I scrutinised her from close range: her skin was perfect, so much better than the times I'd seen her resurrected inside the Nexus. That could only have been because of the blood she'd drunk since her escape. That thought restored memories from Newcastle, the police station and what I'd done there.

A rush of images and sensations threatened to overwhelm me: blood, teeth, falling, exploding light, the flavour of death, then the taste of life, then anger and hate; hate so strong it was only by hanging on to Bella I stayed on my feet. I tried to identify what had produced such a response in me, guessing it was the hatred of taking a life, even a demon one, and a dislike of having to drink that blood.

Then that thought changed and it felt like hatred of something else: something specific - of someone specific. A shadow stumbled around inside my head as I faltered towards the Tube station. It stepped into my light and revealed where the hatred originated: it was for a parent. I knew that without question, but as I was about to dig deeper into my mind, Bella dragged me into reality.

'This is it, Alice.' She let go of me. 'Are you sure you're all right? We can return tomorrow night if you prefer.'

I shook the memories from my head. 'No. We'll do this now.' I wiped at my eyes and gathered my bearings. People milled around outside the station. A bug-eyed man with wild hair harangued the passing public by waving a large placard in the air.

'The end of the world is nigh,' he shouted.

I dodged his outstretched hands and followed Bella into the underground. She whipped out a credit card and pressed it against the gate. Then she handed it to me to do the same when she was on the other side.

'Where did you get this from?' I returned it to her after using it.

She winked at me. 'Same place I got that tasty human blood.'

I pushed back my annoyance and followed her to the platform. The smile on her face, that constant grin indicating she knew things I didn't, left me suddenly reluctant to talk to her. I sulked during the ride to Balham, but it didn't appear to bother Bella, who spent it flirting with any man or woman who caught her eye. It was a tedious journey and I stomped from the carriage when we arrived. I was sixteen, yet I'd never felt like a teenager or a kid before; but I did now. I glared at her while she chatted to a busker near the exit.

'So, where do we go from here?' I was no expert on the London Underground, but I was reasonably sure there were only the platform and the lines where we were.

Bella abandoned the musician. 'This has changed since I was here last.' There was a nervous flicker in her eye. 'I don't have good memories of the place.' She clutched at her heart as she peered at the display showing the Tube times. I followed her further down the platform until we reached the end.

'What now?'

She pulled me from the edge as a train trundled into the station.

'We've got two minutes until the next train.' Bella jumped down to the line behind the last carriage. 'Watch out for the electric line when you get here.' Then she disappeared into the dark.

I peered after her as people scrambled into the Tube train, grabbing seats, putting their heads down and ignoring everything around them. Nobody seemed to notice what we were doing.

'Which one is the electric line?' I yelled after her. There was no reply. I swore under my breath and climbed down, making sure I didn't touch any of the rails. My fingers brushed the walls as I headed into the gloom. The concrete was wet and the air smelled of burning electricity.

'Stick to the side,' Bella shouted into the dark.

As if I had any choice. The ground rumbled beneath my feet as my shoes crunched over small stones. Somewhere ahead of me, I thought I saw her weaving between the lines. Damp dropped from the roof and cold bit at my skin.

'Where are you?' I said as I walked into something.

'You found me.'

'How long do we have to do this?'

'Until we find the Forge's secret lair from 1940. And we need to do it in the next ninety seconds.'

'Why?' I said through gritted teeth.

'Because that's when the latest Tube is due.'

I cursed her name under my breath. 'If you get hit by a train, will you die?'

Bella glanced at me. 'No. You?'

She strode ahead and I resisted the urge to punch her in the back of the neck. The temperature ballooned and the ground rattled beneath me.

'How are we supposed to find this place? Surely it would have been lost to time or the London Underground by now?'

'I can smell a shapeshifter from fifty feet away. This won't be any different.'

As she finished speaking, lights blared ahead of me. The earth shook, and the illumination sped closer. There was no point turning back as death hurtled down a track and straight for me.

I held my breath and waited for the impact.

20 CASSIE: INCURSION

The only windows in the truck were at the front, so it wasn't easy to see what was outside from where I sat in the back. The Special Ops driver and the two next to him spoke in whispers instead of using the comms. Captain Hall inched between them to get a good view.

'Okay, there's nothing out there apart from a light blue covering. It's not as thick as the cloud making up most of the Zone.'

'Can you see where we're headed?' Luke said.

The top of Hall's protective suit shook from side to side. 'No. We're going to have to drive into the mist blind.'

A groan went up from someone as the truck bounced over the ground and we all had to grab the sides to stay upright. Claudia leant into me, so I was squashed against the side of the vehicle. The driver stopped and peered into the blue covering the windscreen.

With all of us compressed inside the back, my brain started to spin as I felt claustrophobic. It was a new sensation to me, and I didn't like it. I scratched at my arm as the irritation grew in my head. I needed to get out. I put my hand on the back door, ready to push it open.

'I'll be back in a few minutes.'

Hall's voice screamed across the comms. 'What are you doing?'

'We can't go forward until we know what's out there. You said this mist wouldn't harm me and the others, so I'll do some recon.'

I exited before he could protest and before any of the blue infiltrated the truck. I slammed the door behind me, glad to be outside, no matter what was waiting inside that haze.

The air was warm as I stepped out. The mist was barely visible where we were; it was like the thin vapour you get on an early autumn morning, one that nips at your legs and leaves them damp. I swept a hand through it, and it dissipated into nothingness; there was no touch or sensation to it, no smell of anything. I wondered if this was some giant hoax or test that Erasmus, Bolt, Hall and the rest of them had planned to punish me for what I'd done to their president and the others I'd killed.

'What's happening, Kane?' Hall's voice was gruff and impatient in my ear.

I moved to the front of the van, peering through the side window to see the driver. I gave him a thumbs up and answered his leader's question.

'We're still in the same field as the tent.' The thin fog covered it. 'Apart from the blue, which is so light you can peer through it, there's nothing here but grass.'

I moved in front of the truck and looked for the forest ahead of us. There was a road through it which ran past a lake, and then we'd be on the edge of Valhalla. After that, it would be another four miles into the centre of the town and

President Dixon's parental home. According to Hall, it was a straight run from where we were.

'What's there, Kane?'

'There's nothing here or up ahead.'

Had Pandora somehow consumed the trees and human life? If she was devouring everything in her way, and we couldn't stop her, America would be desolate in the next twenty-four hours, stripped of every living thing as if infested with the worst swarm of locusts in history.

'You can't see the woods?'

I was about to tell him no when something appeared on the horizon, drifting out of the thicker blue hovering there. A large, darker cloud moved towards us, shimmering and undulating as it approached. I stepped a few feet forward for a better look, but it was the noise which hit me next: a high-pitched shrieking which rattled my ears and must have travelled through my comms device and into the truck, which shook as I fell back and put my hand on the front.

'What the fuck?' It was a combined expletive from everyone in the vehicle.

The shadowy mass heading my way shrieked again. I had my hands over my ears this time, so the damage was reduced, but still, my head ached because of it. An echo of it reverberated inside my skull, kicking against my brain and resurrecting recent memories of hearing a similar, unearthly noise.

I peeled my fingers from my ears and listened again, prepared for the shrieking, but still flinching when it came. And then I remembered what it was.

Harpies.

Shit!

Alice and I had fought them in Limbo and just about escaped with our lives. There were only a few of the creatures then, but as I gazed ahead of me now, I knew there could be hundreds in the approaching dark cloud.

I scrambled back into the van when the screaming was about a hundred yards from me, and everyone looked at me in expectation. Hall should have been the one to give the orders, but I shouted at them as I pushed my way to the front.

'Drive now, as quick as you can.'

The driver stared at me with fear in his eyes. 'It's moving too fast for us to get around or outrun it.'

'You won't do either of those; you need to hit it head-on and power right through the centre.'

All I could see through the windscreen was a thick wall of darkness rushing towards us. Hall saw it too.

'Are you mad?' he said. 'The truck will smash apart if we crash into that.'

I considered telling them what was approaching but thought an attack by hundreds of flying monsters would scramble anyone's brain; it was best to keep them in the dark for as long as possible. But one thing I knew about harpies, from fighting them in Limbo, was as fierce and horrible as they appeared, their bodies were fragile and you could break their bones with little force. Driving straight into them should scatter a good chunk all over this field.

'Drive now; it's the only thing which will save us.'

The driver looked to Hall for confirmation as the shrieking grew loud enough to make the windows tremble. That's when Hall nodded at him.

He didn't need more encouragement, putting his foot down and speeding towards the thick darkness. Then the dark split in half and I saw the horde of wings coming straight for us.

I hoped those behind me couldn't see the blazing red

eyes and glistening teeth waiting for us. As I prepared for the crash, the shrieking grew into a crescendo that shook the truck.

And then it abruptly stopped, with the air silent apart from the sound of the wheels bouncing across the ground and thirteen heartbeats seemingly hissing through our shared communication network.

I grabbed the side of the truck and Claudia gripped onto me as we smashed into the beasts full on. We smacked into each other with the impact. It was only when I got my bearings and peered at what covered the windscreen that I realised it wasn't harpies at all: it was hundreds of birds.

'Pigeons are attacking us,' Claudia shouted at me.

They swamped the van so it was impossible for the driver to see out, but it didn't matter; we had to keep moving and hope we'd scatter them. He did this for about a minute, and then gaps appeared on the windscreen. When only a few pigeons remained, he used the wipers to clean away the blood and the fowl debris. Then it was possible to see the forest.

The crazed birds kept on coming as we moved, bouncing off the sides and the roof as some were squashed under the truck. Once we had a clear view, everyone let out a collective sigh of relief; everyone but me. It couldn't be that easy.

But Captain Hall disagreed. 'We'll have the president out in no time if all we have to worry about is a few manic birds.'

As he spoke, we came to a shuddering halt, throwing everyone into the person opposite. Luke grabbed me, smiling as he did so. He pressed his face close to mine while placing his hand over the microphone attached to his top.

Then he whispered to me, 'This guy in charge will get us all killed.'

I was about to agree when we fell back into our seats and I slipped from Luke's arms. He was opposite me once more, but I still felt his touch around me.

Hall spoke again. 'What's happened, Johnson?'

I assumed he was talking to the driver, who replied.

'The engine has stalled, Captain. I think birds have got under the hood and clogged it up.'

'Great.' Hall's voice trembled on that one word. Even inside his hazmat suit, sweat was visible swimming down his forehead. He looked around the back of the truck. The shrieking had stopped and it was silent outside. 'Someone has to check the engine.'

Claudia piped up. 'Why don't you do it, Hall? Then you can test your uniform to see if it works.'

'I'm in charge here, vampire.' Behind the plastic, his eyes glowered at her. 'So maybe I'll send you.'

She threw up her hands. 'I'm a sixteen-year-old girl. What do I know about engines?'

Hall was continuing to mull over who he was about to force outside when Colleen got up.

'I'll do it.'

I put my hand on her. 'We'll do it together.'

'Then be quick about it,' Hall shouted.

We squeezed through the others and exited the van. The cobalt mist was thicker, but nothing that would affect breathing or movement. There was no sign of birds anywhere, the air heavy with silence. Colleen stuck out her arm and watched the blue settle on her skin.

'It doesn't feel of anything,' she said.

I grabbed her hand and we went to the front of the truck.

'We're on the outskirts of Pandora's power here; it'll be worse the further we get into the town.' I let go of her and got hold of the bonnet. 'When I lift this, if something flies out, you deal with it, okay?'

'With all your abilities, can't you handle a few birds?'

'I doubt what attacked us were normal pigeons. Are you ready?'

She nodded and I pulled it open. Nothing came out, but I didn't get too close. I'd played around with a few motor engines in my time, so I had a good idea of what to look for. I leant over and found what I wanted: the body of a dead pigeon stuck in the engine. I picked it out, checked there weren't any others, and tossed it to the side.

'Is it done?' Colleen said.

'I think so.' I looked at the driver. 'Give it a go now.'

He did and it started. I closed the bonnet as the squeal came from behind us. Colleen dragged me to the ground as the birds missed us by inches; my back pushed into the grass as I peered into the sky. A dozen pigeons hovered there, with heads so twisted and disfigured there was no doubt something malevolent possessed them. They glared at me with malign intelligence beaming from their faces; they waited to make their next attack as Colleen gripped on to me. I lifted slightly, never taking my gaze from the flock, and pressed into her.

'I'll distract them while you run for the truck.'

She shook her head. 'It's my turn to play the hero.' The birds swooped in one large mass as Colleen stuck her face towards them. 'Stick your fingers in your ears, Cassie.'

As soon as I did, she let rip a screech louder than anything I'd ever heard before. Even with my hands over my head, my skull vibrated as if a train was running over it. Blood slipped between my fingers and out of my nose as I watched the birds plunge before bursting apart in one fell swoop. Blood, guts and feathers flew everywhere as Colleen pulled me over and we rolled away from most of the avian damage. Bits of dead pigeons rained down around me as she hauled me up.

'Thanks,' I said. She dug into her ear and threw the damaged communicator to the floor.

'None of this is any good now.'

I did the same as we returned to the truck. 'At least we won't have Hall shouting in our heads anymore.'

Colleen put her hand on my arm before I opened the door. 'If Pandora can do that to the birds, what's she done to every other living thing in that town?'

I tried not to imagine it.

And we still had to get through the forest.

21 ALICE: FORGE

Blaring lights and sounds came rushing towards me. I thought about running to the platform, but knew I wouldn't make it in time. The air smelt of burning rubber and the hairs bristled on my arm. At the back of my throat, there was a lingering taste of demon blood, and I pictured teleporting out of the underground.

Then metal brushed against my leg as my face kissed damp concrete. The wall split apart and I fell forward. My nose hit hard ground and I struggled to breathe. The room stank of old papers and unwashed clothes as I pressed my hands into the cold floor.

Bella lifted me.

Her teeth sparkled white as she spoke.

'Well, that was a close call. Are you okay?'

'I'm regretting freeing you from the Nexus.'

She let go of my arm and I stumbled into a table of newspapers that fell to the ground as I regained my balance. She held up her hands and glanced around the room.

'Why would you say that when I've brought you to the Promised Land?'

I picked up a newspaper. It was from 1976 and screamed out to me about the filth and the fury.

'Where are we, Bella?'

'This is the lair of the Forge.' She looked at every inch of the place. 'They don't appear to be here, but all we have to do is wait.'

My heart continued to thump against my ribs at a hundred beats a second as I looked around the room. I grabbed a bunch of papers and scanned through the headlines and dates.

'It doesn't look like anyone's been here for decades. What makes you believe they'll turn up now?'

Bella sat on a sofa and a torrent of dust swirled into the air.

'Unlike you, Alice, I'm an eternal optimist. How else do you think I survived in the Nexus all those years?'

I brushed off her insult and looked around the secret place. It was well lit, with a fold-up bed, a toilet and sink, and magazines and newspapers scattered everywhere. An ancient radio and tape deck sat rusting in the corner while empty crisp packets and sweet papers stuck to the floor. There was a pile of dusty clothes at the back, and I ignored the temptation to go through them.

'How did you know this would be here?'

She shrugged. 'I smelt the anti-life seeping through the walls. Then we got lucky and found the right pressure point to get inside.'

'What would have happened if it hadn't been here, the hidden door to the secret room?'

Bella shook her head. 'What do you mean, Alice?'

I spoke through gritted teeth. 'There was a train speeding towards us if you remember. How would we have dealt with that?'

'Oh, that. Well, my reflexes are back to normal, so I'd have jumped to the ceiling and clung there until it passed.'

'What about me?'

She grinned at me. 'I'm sure your innate Arcane abilities would have kicked in and saved you somehow.'

I had to stop myself from biting through my tongue and focused on why we were there.

'So we'll wait until this Nazi supernatural super-soldier turns up?'

She pointed to a stack of books behind me. 'We could read their diaries while we're here.'

I grabbed the top volume and wiped the filth from it. 'How do you know they're diaries?'

'If you were in here on your own for decades, what would you write about?'

I opened it and leafed through the first few pages.

'It's all in German.'

'Good job I'm fluent in twenty languages, then.' Bella held out her hand. 'Give it to me.'

I passed it to her. She delved into it in a frenzy, flicking through it like an animated cartoon.

'What does it say?'

'It would appear our super-duper shapeshifter has had many names: Lulu, Bruce, Greta, Rudolph, Ayesha, Oscar, and even Isabella. This is their life story since the day of their birth in a Nazi lab. There's a list of the famous here, including Clement Attlee, Vivien Leigh, Hitchcock, Brian Epstein, Diana Dors, George Best, Brian Jones, Barbara Castle, Joe Orton, Johnny Rotten, George Michael, and David Cameron.'

I held on to the grubby chair opposite her. 'Are you saying this shapeshifter was all these people?'

'Perhaps they were, or they were someone close to them.' She continued to look through the pages.

'Was this all part of a Nazi plan after the war?'

Bella scrunched up her face and shook her head. 'According to this, they were anti-Nazi from the start, but kept this from their fascist masters. From the first moment they stepped into Britain, they did all they could to stop Hitler's plans.' She turned over more pages and looked through other diaries. 'Then they continued to live their life and assimilate into human society the best they could. It would seem our Nazi supernatural shape-shifting super-soldier became a pillar of British life. They even paid their taxes on time.'

None of this made me feel any better. 'How is this going to help us?'

'I've no idea, but it's fascinating how our presumptions suddenly become something different.'

I kicked over a pile of old newspapers and slumped onto a creaking sofa.

'You're doing this on purpose so I'll drink more demon blood.'

Bella removed the phial from her jacket and held it out to me.

'Far from it, Alice. I'm as surprised as you by what we've found here, but if you want to take matters into your own hands, I'll bow down to your will.'

I stared at the red liquid as it shimmered inside the glass. What was I prepared to do to see my sister again and rescue my mother?

Before I could decide, the answer was taken from me.

'I knew someone would find me, eventually.'

The voice shocked me to my senses. I jumped up and turned towards the entrance. A woman stood in the doorway, over six feet tall with beautiful skin, sparkling brown eyes, and the greatest afro hair ever. She was like an African Amazon sprung to life, and she looked very familiar.

The blade was in my hand, my body ready to leap into action. Bella appeared unconcerned, lounging around and picking fluff from her nails.

'You don't look like a Nazi.'

Sweat glistened on the woman's lips. 'I never was.' Pain crisscrossed her face. 'When the bomb distracted my watchers, I slipped from them for the first time since they stole my sister and me from our parents.' She gazed at Bella. 'I remember you from that night in the Tube station, seeing you on the platform before the world collapsed around us.'

Bella sat up straight. 'I was searching for you.' She patted her heart. 'Until fate intervened.'

The tension in the room evaporated, and to be honest, most of it had been coming from me. I peered at this woman and saw no threat.

'Are you Forge?' I said.

She grimaced. 'That was the stupid title Himmler gave me. My name is Angie.'

'That's Bella, and I'm Alice. Will you tell us what happened to you? You said you have a sister?'

Sadness engulfed Angie's face. 'My twin sister, Freda. I don't know what happened to her after Mengele separated us.'

Bella's eyes widened. 'Dr Josef Mengele, the Nazi Angel of Death?'

'That was him. He was obsessed with identical twins, so Freda and I received special attention because we were part of, in his words, the inferior batch.' She walked across the dirty floor towards the long mirror at the end of the room. Groups of photographs were stuck to the glass, images of the famous I recognised mixed in with snaps of ordinary people I didn't. She opened a drawer and removed a faded black-and-white photo, and handed it to me. It was cracked and wrinkled against my fingers. Peering from the image were identical twin girls, maybe ten years old, with beaming parents standing behind them.

'Is this you and your family?'

Angie nodded. 'It was taken two years before our house was burned to the ground. After that, I never saw my mother and father again. Freda and I were transported from one camp to another until we ended up in Mengele's laboratory. So many had died before us.' She paused and took a long breath. 'Sometimes, I wished I'd joined them. But Freda kept me going. She was always the stronger of us.'

Bella was by my side before I noticed she'd moved. There was genuine empathy on her face.

'Can you talk about the experiments?'

Angie removed her jacket. She wore a short-sleeved purple top and held her arm out.

'What you see now is the real me, but there are two things I keep hidden from the rest of the world.'

Her skin was beautiful, with an unblemished luminescence magnetic to the eyes. The back of her elbow, which a tattoo artist once described to me as the Ditch, shimmered. It glowed for a second before changing into ravaged flesh, where dozens of needles must have penetrated at some time. Then she bent to reveal the same thing on the rear of her neck.

My fingers grasped for my lips. 'Oh my God.'

Angie snapped her head back. 'I don't know how many died before me, but I think I was one of the few to survive.'

'They injected you with shapeshifter blood?' Bella said.

'They did that to me and numerous others, including Freda.'

I placed my hand on her arm. 'What happened to her?'

There were tears in her eyes as she spoke. 'I don't know. After the war, I went back to Germany to find Freda and my parents. I discovered my mother and father had been in the same concentration camp up to the outbreak of the war. Then, sometime in 1940, they were placed on different trains and disappeared into Eastern Europe.' She dried her cheeks. 'I scoured every archive in Germany and Russia, infiltrated American and British military intelligence, but I found no trace of them.'

Pain gripped my heart. 'And Freda?'

'She vanished with Mengele. She either went with him as Germany burned, or she was something he covered up.' Angie turned to Bella. 'So, I had no love for the Nazis. When the bomb dropped on the Tube station and it flooded, it was easy to slip away from the SS officers assigned to handle me. Then I changed into whoever I wanted, and they couldn't find me.'

'What did you do then?' Bella said.

'My first thought was to escape and hide. I was only fourteen, on my own in war-torn London. I couldn't be myself for a long time.' She placed the family photo back in the drawer. 'For five years, I became a succession of orphaned British children joining the evacuee programmes, which transported kids from the most dangerous areas of the land and into the countryside. I grew up quickly over those five years.

'Then, when the war was over, I attached myself to the British unit assigned to deal with Nazi war criminals. I spent time at Nuremberg, interrogating Goering and Speer under the guise of British intelligence, before making my way into Stalin's Soviet territories. It was a fruitless search through a never-ending sea of atrocities.'

She finished and clutched at her chest. I got the impression she'd wanted to tell someone this for a long time.

Bella peered straight at her. 'Why did you return here?'

'After Eastern Europe, I travelled through North and South America, my appearance changing with the times and the place I was in, but I never felt settled. I met other shapeshifters and supernatural creatures, but they knew I was different and said I wasn't pure in their eyes. I was an experiment to them, a half-breed. They either shunned me or tried to kill me. So I kept on moving.' She glanced around the room. 'I was reborn here, so this is where I belonged.' She looked at Bella, and then at me. 'And now you're here to kill me.'

I strode forward and took her hands in mine.

'No. We're here to ask for your help. I can't find my mother and my sister without you.'

She gazed into my face, and then buried her head in my shoulder. We stayed like that for a minute before she let go. Her eyes were red raw as she spoke.

'Tell me what you need.'

22 CASSIE: A FOREST

Once we were back in the truck, everyone dispensed with their damaged comms. Hall didn't look too happy, unable to bark orders into our ears, but the rest seemed pleased we'd survived our first attack from Pandora. I only hoped they didn't think it would get any easier from here.

Sayan was sitting with her eyes closed while Wovoka whispered something to Luke. Allister was opposite me, biting his nails as if he hadn't eaten for days. None of them appeared too disturbed by what we'd just been through.

Luke must have been reading my thoughts.

'They were only pigeons, Cassie. Yes, there were a lot of them, but it wasn't anything we couldn't handle.'

I didn't bother with a reply, instead focusing on what other threats we might face.

With the vehicle decluttered from demonic birds, we drove on and took the road through the forest. Hall scrutinised a small map as we travelled.

Claudia gripped my hand. 'Are you all right?'

I glanced at Colleen sitting opposite. 'I am thanks to my Irish friend.'

The banshee tilted her head at me. 'Maybe next time you'll let me smoke when I want.'

Against my better judgement, considering our present and likely future circumstances, I laughed.

'Okay, I will.' I noticed the blue outside getting thicker the further we went into it. 'And we don't have those irritating bits of plastic in our ears anymore.'

Colleen grinned. 'And it was all thanks to a flock of crazed birds.'

Claudia released my hand. 'I met Hitchcock once, you know.' Colleen and I looked at her. 'It was in London before he was famous. He was working at *The Henley Telegraph* and he printed one of my short stories.'

This revelation was more shocking to me than being attacked by zombie pigeons.

'You're a writer?'

She held up her hands and shrugged. 'Well, I dabble, but I wouldn't say I'm a writer.' She scrunched her lips together and appeared every bit the teenager she wasn't. 'Though I have met a few famous authors over the years. I'll tell you some tales to make your toes curl when we get out of this place.'

I looked at her and I was glad to see her smiling, even in our current treacherous situation. Those memories of hers I'd stumbled across while inside her mind made my skin shiver every time I thought of them, so they must have been a terrible burden for her.

'We're entering the forest,' Hall shouted through the truck as I noticed Luke observing me; it was a look I assumed meant 'I'm glad you're okay'. I studied him as we kept moving, trying to guess his age: twenty-one, twenty-two maybe.

Claudia pressed her lips to my ear. 'He's a bit of a looker, isn't he, with those dreamy eyes and cheekbones you could fall asleep in.'

I pushed her from me. 'Don't be daft.'

'You know, when this is over, perhaps you and he should get together and relax a little. I'm sure you could do with it.'

'The first thing I'm going to do after this is find Alice and my mother.'

'Yes, of course, but don't deny yourself a bit of fun as well. I mean, that dishy dust devil is boring into you with those gorgeous peepers of his.'

I was about to tell her off when something substantial smashed into the truck and everyone opposite flew at us. Colleen landed on me, and then fell to the side as Luke rolled over and ended up in my arms. We were squeezed together, chest to chest when an object hit the back, and we all went into the other side. The vehicle wobbled on its wheels for a few seconds before levelling out.

'What's happening?' Hall shouted.

We were stationary and catching our breath when another attack smashed into the rear and the door buckled. No one had time to respond before something crashed through the windscreen and dragged the driver out. My head was pinned to the metal behind me as I watched the two passengers follow, pulled out so quickly I didn't see what did it.

Everyone froze, me included, as gunfire erupted outside, followed by the unmistakable sound of screaming. However, it wasn't that which broke the spell, but the destruction of the truck's back door. Colleen was at it in a flash, her mouth open as I covered my ears; still, her shriek penetrated my head and made the rest of me tremble.

I don't know if it lasted a second or a minute, as the next thing I knew, she was hauling me outside. We landed in the forest and the others followed. Claudia was on one side of me, Luke on the other, with all of us staring at a sight from a horror movie: three giant bears held the troops from the truck between their clawed fingers.

Colleen let go of me. 'I hate fucking bears.'

Before we could react, the animals tore the soldiers apart, ripping arms and legs from their bodies and tossing them aside like rag dolls. I turned to see where the rest of the team was, finding them all gone. I didn't blame them.

'Time to show us your beautiful singing voice again, Red,' Claudia said.

Colleen shook her head as the beasts growled and slavered at us.

'Two heavy bursts in quick succession have burnt me out, kid. I need about fifteen minutes to get my breath back.'

That was time these bears weren't about to give us. The animals turned to each other, and I could have sworn they communicated in some silent manner. As I wondered what to do, Luke stepped forward and thrust his hands at them. He was all fingers and thumbs, his flesh vibrating and shimmering as he pulled up every piece of dirt and dust nearby. Then he flicked his arms out and what he'd gathered smashed into the heads of the possessed animals, collecting there and swirling into their eyes, mouths, ears, and up their noses. I imagined it travelling down into their lungs and piercing their hearts. Within thirty seconds, they'd stopped moving and toppled over with a loud crash.

Luke froze, his face glazed, ready to slump to the ground before Colleen and I caught him.

She winked at me. 'I saw him first, kid.'

We pulled him up and stumbled back to the vehicle. There was still no sign of the others. We sat Luke on the edge of the truck and I touched his face.

'Luke, are you okay?'

His eyes flashed awake, his shoulders slumped. 'I am now.' He gazed at me. Then he wiped at his head. 'I shouldn't be this tired.' He stared at his palms. 'It feels like I've been doing that for twelve hours.'

I peered at the swirling blue around us and noticed how it had become thicker the further we got inside the Zone.

'I think it's this place doing it to you, draining your abilities somehow. It was the same for Colleen.'

Claudia floated about eight feet off the ground. 'I believe you're right, Cassie. I can't go any higher than this.'

'So, what does that mean for you, Cassandra Kane?'

The demon had returned with the others; they all appeared sheepish apart from him.

'Where did you lot get to?'

'Discretion is the better part of valour. Captain Hall decided it was best to retreat while we assessed the situation. I thought it was an excellent decision, and no one disagreed.'

I looked at Hall as he hung his head. Then I spoke to Sayan and Wovoka.

'Do you feel weaker inside the Zone?'

Wovoka held up his hands. 'I won't know until I perform the Ghost Dance, and I can't do that until I get close to the source of this disturbance in nature.'

And that meant finding Pandora. I turned to the shamanka.

'What about you, Sayan?'

She walked forward and strode towards the remains of the Special Ops.

'The spirits of the bears cry out in pain, tortured by what she did to them.' Sayan glanced at the human body parts. 'The soldiers are lost, trying to gather their souls for the journey to the next world.' Then she turned to me. 'Only death surrounds you, child.'

She stepped past me and knelt at the head of a bear. I left her to it and went to the others. I ignored Hall and spoke to the two remaining Special Ops.

'Can one of you drive the truck?'

They looked at it, standing there with the front smashed in, both sides dented to Hell, and the back ripped out. The woman replied.

'Sure, if it still works.'

'What's your name?' I asked her.

'Brooks,' she said. 'Eva Brooks.'

'Okay, Eva; see what condition it's in.' I left her to it while I gathered Colleen, Claudia, and Luke together. The two mystics strode around the dead while the demon bit his lips and peered at me. 'Are you feeling better, Luke?'

If he wasn't, could we keep the blue mist at bay when we got to the centre of Valhalla?

He rubbed at the back of his neck and stood. 'Yeah, I think so. I was just surprised such a little thing knocked me out like that.'

'That was no little thing,' Claudia said. 'You saved us all.'

Eva returned before Luke spoke. 'It'll be a bumpy ride, but it should get us there.'

'That's unlucky thirteen down to ten, then.' Allister picked at his teeth as he joined us. The medicine man and the shamanka came over, leaving only Captain Hall near the trees. If there were more dangers in there, he didn't seem too bothered. The demon must have seen me staring at Hall. 'I'm not sure how much use he'll be to us now.' He flicked his toothpick into the ground. As it landed in the grass, I noticed the red stain on it. 'Perhaps this would be a good time to take the trigger from him.'

'Let's see, shall we?'

I strode towards Hall, leaving the others opened mouthed, but they soon followed, with Claudia catching up first.

'What are you going to do, Cassie?' She wasn't afraid, only excited.

'Watch.' Hall's fingers shook as I approached, his lips mumbling inside his protective suit. I held out my hand. 'Give me the triggering device for the explosives, Captain.'

He looked incredulous as he backed into a tree. Then he pulled out what I'd asked for and placed a finger over the screen. He brushed it and a warm sensation invaded my throat. I twisted my head to see six red lights flickering.

'If you come any closer, I'll press this.'

I stared straight into that suit. 'And who'll save Dixon then?'

He sneered through the plastic covering his face. 'I don't care. He's not my president. I voted for the guy you killed, monster girl.'

'You wanted him to start a nuclear war, didn't you?'

'I should have been in that bunker with him.' He glared at me. 'I would have stopped you.'

'I doubt it, soldier boy.'

Claudia dropped from the air above him and snatched the trigger from his hand. He floundered forward as she handed the device to me. I stepped to the side as Hall fell flat on his face. I waited for Brooks and the other Special Op to come over and help him, but they didn't. I watched him struggle to get up and held the remote in the air.

'If you want it so badly, Captain, then I'll do it for you.'

Then I pressed the digital button.

23 ALICE: THE PALACE

I t took me thirty minutes to tell Angie the story of my family, of preventing the end of the world and how we had to get inside Buckingham Palace to find Dracula and my mother.

'You're a Child of the Arcane?'

'It appears so.'

'The Nazis spoke about the Nephilim. I know Himmler sent people to scour the planet for them, but I thought they were a myth.' Angie grasped my hand and pulled me towards the mirror. 'Do you want to see how my powers work?'

'Will it hurt?'

She smiled at me. 'No one's ever complained before.' She peered into the photos dotted around the glass. 'Who would you like to be, Alice?'

I glanced at Bella. 'Make me her.'

Angie laughed. 'Okay.'

She removed her hand and placed her fingers on my face; they were warm to the touch and smelt of ice cream. Her flesh trembled against mine. Skin pressed up to skin, my pores glued to hers.

It was my insides I felt changing at first. When I'd drunk the Demon Lord's blood, it had burnt from my organs outwards, searing my veins and bones as it consumed my skull. It only left me when I started throwing up. This was different. My skin tingled, but not unpleasantly. It was as if I was in a Jacuzzi and warm water rippled against my flesh.

As I adjusted to the sensation, I gazed into the mirror. My face wobbled, shimmered, and transformed. I was no longer Alice, but Bella, only slightly younger and more confused. I placed my hand to my cheek, touching the different me and enjoying it. It was the first time I'd looked into a mirror and liked what I saw.

Bella peered at me with no reflection of her in the glass.

'I'd forgotten how good looking I am.'

I ran my fingers over my new face. 'This is amazing.' Imagine being whoever you want to be, to cleansing every single imperfection. For a second, I craved to lose myself in anyone else, to be anyone else, until I remembered Cassie was lost somewhere in the world. 'How long does it last?'

Angie stared at me. 'It depends with other people; an hour at the max, usually. What is it you want to do?'

I'd told her about getting into Buckingham Palace and my current situation as a wanted fugitive.

'Make me anonymous, but we'll need you with us to get inside.'

'The official reception is tomorrow, but there's a gathering there tonight,' Angie said.

Bella stared into the mirror and touched a cheek she couldn't see.

'How do you know this?'

'Nothing escapes me in this city.'

'Is that how you knew we were here?' I said.

She grinned. 'I have an alarm linked to my phone. As soon as you stepped through the door, I headed here.'

'Weren't you afraid?' I said. 'About what you'd find here.'

Angie shook her head. 'My curiosity always gets the better of me.'

'How will you get us inside the Royal Palace?' Bella said.

It was hard for me to focus on anything but my resemblance to a young Bella reflected in the mirror.

'I'll become one of the younger Royals and lead you straight through the gates. It won't be the first time I've done it.' She turned to me. 'It all depends on who you need to be.' She glanced at Bella. 'I'm guessing you don't want to look like the baby vampire?' She touched my cheek. It shimmered and rippled, and in the reflection, I returned to myself. I was disappointed and relieved in unison.

My fingertips caressed my face as my heart ached at the thought of my missing sister. Was it fate I'd ended up in the bowels of the London Underground, hoping a separated twin would lead me to Cassie?

'Make me as unassuming as you can,' I said to her.

My shoulders slumped as my arms went limp.

Bella came to my side. 'This is good, Alice. It won't be long until you're reunited with your mother, and then you can journey to America to find your sister.'

I took Angie's hand in mine. 'Will you come with me?'

Angie ran a hand through her Afro. 'Nothing could stop me.'

She placed her other hand on my face once more. The process felt like my head was in a gentle whirlpool, my skin rippling as if covered by warm water. My cheekbones and nose moulded like putty, but wasn't painful or unpleasant.

Instead, invisible hands reshaped my features and it felt strangely therapeutic.

When I gazed in the mirror, I was the complete opposite of me: short blonde hair, brown eyes, and freckled cheeks. Again, I was glad to be anyone but me.

We were three amigos, three sisters ready to right the wrongs done to us. I held both their hands in mine and gazed into the glass. Angie was beautiful, I was a stranger, and Bella was an empty space.

'So how do we get to Buckingham Palace?' I said.

Bella grinned and spoke for all of us. 'With great optimism.'

Leaving the underground bunker was less dangerous than getting in. Angie knew a more accessible route in the opposite direction to how we'd got there. It was a short walk between the lines and a hidden set of stairs up. It was still night when we emerged above ground, which Bella was pleased about.

'I'm not walking there,' she said.

Angie had a phone in her hand. 'Don't worry; a taxi will suffice.'

The ride took fewer than twenty minutes, the three of us squeezed into the back like mates ready for a party on the town; not that I knew how that felt. I'd never had friends before meeting Cassie, and Medusa was only an online one because of the circumstances. And I'd never been on a night out with anyone; never been a girl who laughed in the right places and attracted the wrong glances.

I'm not sure if the driver could hear us, but I'm guessing if he could, he'd have eavesdropped on to some of the strangest stories ever spoken in that cab. In that short drive, Bella regaled us with a tale of Berlin in the 1920s; Angie recounted how she'd sat as a model for Salvador Dali; while

I mentioned how I'd accidentally poisoned an angel in Hollywood. By the time we arrived at Buckingham Palace, we were like long-lost friends.

The driver dropped us outside the gates and Angie paid him. Glamour and glitz were everywhere, but it meant nothing to me. I'd walked through streets littered with the homeless, lived with people who struggled with their thoughts and received no support, and rubbed shoulders with those who'd run out of money before the end of the first week of the month. This heritage and privilege were meaningless to me.

Angie thrust her hand through the gates and waved at the security. Only she wasn't Angie; she was someone in line for the throne who would never get the chance to sit on it. A uniformed man ran towards us, his cheeks flushed and eyes apologetic.

'My Lady, I'm sorry you've been left outside. Nobody informed me you were coming.'

Angie gave him her best fake smile through her false face as he opened the gates.

'Don't worry. I wanted to keep it on the QT.'

We followed her into the grounds, watching as members of the public took photos and videos. My heart was pressed against my lungs in the anticipation my facade would collapse at any moment and reveal my true self.

The security man fell over backwards to get us inside and away from the riff-raff outside.

Angie grabbed his hand as we entered the building.

'You've been too kind. I'll take it from here.'

She left him behind without a second glance while we stuck to her shadow.

Then I snatched her arm and pulled her back. 'Slow down. We need to work out where we're going.'

She stared at me. 'And where will that be?'

I turned to Bella. 'Do you know where your brother is?'

Bella put a hand to her head. 'I can sense him in my mind, but I can't pinpoint where he is.'

'Christ!' I slapped the wall behind me. 'This place is huge. We'll never find him by stumbling into every room at random.'

'That's why you need an angel's help, ladies.'

I turned around to see Lucy grinning at me.

Bella leapt at her, with fangs bared and hands aiming for her throat. Lucy waved her fingers and Bella froze in the air. Angie and I stood glued to the spot, but it had nothing to do with the First of the Fallen.

'What do you want?' It was all I could think to say. There were others in the Palace, but we appeared to be invisible to them.

Lucy moved at incredible speed, her hand on my cheek before I knew it, her eyes gazing deep into mine.

'You've been drinking poison.' Her smile cut into me. 'And you're not yourself, Alice.'

I slapped her away from me. 'Why do you care?'

'You'll kill yourself if you keep consuming demon blood.' She turned to the motionless Bella. Lucy blinked and Bella dropped to the floor. 'I assume this was your doing?'

'I've helped Alice, unlike you.'

I waited for the argument, but instead, Lucy switched to Angie and held out her hand.

'We haven't met before. I'm Lucy.'

I pulled Angie to one side. 'No more deception, Lucy. Why are you here?'

'What you and Cassie did with the leaders of the free world has led to some unforeseen consequences. The humans are organising on a grand scale, but they've split into different factions.'

For once, I felt as if I was ahead of the game. 'I know all this. Some people want to embrace the supernatural into human society, while others plan to weaponise it. What side are you on?'

Lucy waved her fingers in the air. 'I'm on neither side. I prefer things to remain as they are. The less humanity knows about the likes of us, the better it is for me. That's why I'm here. Imagine my surprise when I saw you walk through the gates.'

'Me?'

She rolled her eyes at me. 'Your disguise doesn't fool me. After all, I am the Queen of Lies.'

For once, her words made me smile. 'So we should believe you now?'

Before Lucy replied, Bella spoke.

'What is my brother up to?'

Lucy spun on her heels. 'Isabella. How long has it been?'

Something unknown punched me in the gut. 'You two know each other?'

Bella looked sheepish. 'We had, err, you know, a thing, some time ago.'

Lucy beamed. 'It was glorious.' She winked at me. 'And it was never just a thing.' She turned to Bella. 'For me.'

I grabbed Bella and Angie, dragging them from the Queen of Lies. Palace guests and staff continued to walk around us, seemingly unaware of the drama in their midst. I let go of Angie and pushed Bella against a suit of armour. The clatter of flesh on metal did nothing to distract our unknowing hosts.

'What else aren't you telling me?' My heartbeat rose and my temperature increased.

'Probably many things, Alice, but none of it matters now.' She glanced over at Lucy. 'The important thing is if you trust her or not.'

I glared at Bella. 'I don't know who to trust.'

Lucy was next to me without moving. 'Not wanting to interrupt, ladies, but time isn't on our side.' She held out her hands and looked around. 'There's a plot afoot to use the image and influence of the Royal Family to reveal the truth about the supernatural to the human world. It's the start of an information war to garner hearts and minds, and whoever fires the first shot controls the narrative.'

'And that's why my brother is here?' Bella said.

A look of utter surprise overtook Lucy. 'Oh, Dracula's not the mastermind behind this plot. I thought you were here because you know who is.' She turned to me. 'It's your mother, Alice, doing this. Mary Arcane is about to reveal one of the Royal Family as a werewolf, and then watch the chaos ensue.'

24 CASSIE: VALHALLA

I wasn't sure who screamed first, but I think it might have been Allister. Then the questions came when nothing happened. Claudia pressed her fingers into the blinking light at her throat when she spoke.

'What did you do, Cassie?'

'Me? Nothing; poor Hall just couldn't keep up his little charade forever.'

'What do you mean?'

I tossed the device into the forest. 'Digital devices don't work inside the Zone, not fully anyway. So all he could do with that trigger was set the red lights off.'

The demon strode towards me, purple anger seeping from his eyes. 'You could have killed us all, taking a risk like that.'

'There was no risk. As soon as I witnessed him using a physical map in the truck and not the GPS on his phone, I knew something was up. And then I remembered there were no electronic devices in the tent either, and there has been no film or video surveillance from inside the Zone since the beginning. Section 25, or at least Olivia Erasmus, continues to receive communications from the Zone, but I don't know how.' I looked at Hall. 'Do you?'

'Fuck you, monster girl.' He staggered by me and into the back of the truck.

Colleen spoke up. 'Can we trust him?'

I went to the passenger seat. 'I've never trusted him.'

The rest followed, with the silence in the vehicle sharp enough to cut through wood. It was a bumpy ride out of the forest, but there were no more attacks from possessed animals. We drove along the road past a clear lake until we reached the entrance to the town, speeding by a sign claiming the population for Valhalla was 4,732.

'I wonder how many are still alive.' Claudia had climbed into the front next to me.

'We'll soon find out.'

We continued through the outskirts until we came to a small industrial park. Chemical and steel plants stood idle as we went further into the blue, the mist getting thicker with every mile we travelled. By the time we got to the centre of the town, it was hard to see more than fifty yards in front of us.

Brooks pulled up near a fast-food joint. 'It's too dangerous to carry on.'

She was right, but it would be much more hazardous once we stepped outside. I turned to those in the back.

'Okay, we stick to the plan.' I waited for Hall to protest and claim he was still in charge, but he sat in silence. 'Luke, try to keep the mist at least five feet away on either side. I know they said it wouldn't affect most of us, but there's no point taking the risk if we can avoid it. Sayan and Wovoka, do your thing as soon as possible. The rest of us are on sentry duty protecting the others.' I looked across at Brooks. 'Do you know where the Dixon family home is?'

She removed a small map from her hazmat pocket. 'We all got these.' She opened it. 'Once we find the town library, we follow the road to the end; it's the last property on the left.'

It sounded a lot simpler than I expected it to be.

We exited the truck together, peering into the haze. When I held my hand out this time, the mist settled on my palm; it appeared as if my flesh was blue.

'We look like Smurfs,' Claudia said.

'Or creatures from that movie, *Avatar*,' Luke said.

Claudia floated two feet off the ground. 'I've had a crush on Sigourney Weaver forever.'

'I'm surprised you haven't met her,' I said while scanning the area.

'Oh, I could have, many times.' Her head disappeared into the thick azure above, only her legs remaining visible. Her voice still drifted down. 'I was working on the set of *Alien* in 1978 in London when I first saw her, well before she became famous. But I've always been too nervous to talk to her.' Then the whole of her vanished into the haze. 'I love her to death.'

I tried not to think of alien killing machines. 'What can you see, Claudia?'

'Nothing; only more of this blue crap. It's thicker up here and it feels oppressive as if it wants to rush down my throat and choke me.'

She dropped to the ground before I told her to get down. I nodded at Luke. He held out his shimmering hands and the mist drifted away, retreating further back until we saw our surroundings: a coffee shop, a bookstore, clothes shops, and the police station.

He stared at me. 'This is okay, better than it was in the woods.'

'Great, keep it up as long as you can.'

'This is the place.' I turned to see Wovoka with his hands in the air. 'The spirits are strong here.' His eyes were black when he looked at me. 'She is nearby, so we have to do this now.'

I nodded. 'Tell us what you need.'

'You must form a circle around me while I perform the Ghost Dance. Then, one of you will sing for me.'

'Sing what?'

'Anything; it doesn't matter.'

Claudia stepped up. 'That's my job then.'

I spoke to Brooks. 'Do you know where this library is?'

She peered into the space Luke had made through the blue haze and pointed forward.

'I'm sure it's down there, on the corner. Can you see the sign with a kid reading on it?'

Her eyesight must have been a lot better than mine, but I took her word for it. That meant four of us to find the house, while six stayed there. Luke could be one of the five in the circle with Claudia, plus Sayan. Now I had to pick two more to remain behind.

I spoke to the other Special Op.

'What's your name?'

'Sergeant Cave, ma'am.'

'Okay, less of the ma'am nonsense. What's your first name, Sergeant?'

'It's Tom.'

I addressed them all. 'I'll find the Dixon house with Hall, Allister, and Colleen. The rest of you stay here and protect each other. We'll return as soon as we locate the president.'

The demon was at my shoulder as I stepped in the direction Brooks had pointed.

'You don't need me, Cassandra. I'd be much better off protecting the others.'

The blue slipped towards us as we walked, thick and heavy in the air. It had a particular aroma, smelling like strawberries for some strange reason. I didn't look at the demon as I spoke.

'I don't trust you or Hall, so you're both coming with me.' I glanced at Colleen. 'And if you step out of line, I know someone who'll blow you away.'

As we headed down the street, all I heard was Claudia singing the opening bars of *Ziggy Stardust*.

Captain Hall crept to my other side. 'What's your plan when we find Dixon? Will you teleport him out of here?'

'You can teleport?' Colleen and Allister said in unison.

'She can do a lot more than that, our little British girl. If you don't watch out, she'll kill you with her mind.'

'If I could do that, you and the demon would have died as soon as we stepped off that plane. And if I could teleport, I would have done so long before Erasmus forced me into this.'

'What are you talking about?'

We strode past a bar and a shoe shop. The mist was closing in, limiting our visibility to about twenty feet. The library was less than a minute away, and then hopefully, the Dixon house would be there. The blue was so thick behind us, there was no way to see the others. Yet I heard Claudia singing.

The demon's hand was on my shoulder. 'Yes, Cassandra Kane; what are you on about?'

I stopped walking and shrugged him off. 'We haven't got time for this because the haze will be so heavy soon, we won't know where we're going.' I stared into the demon's eyes, recognising the malevolence there. 'Whatever abilities I had are gone, so get over it.'

I ran for the library sign. I wasn't sure if the other three would follow, but they did. Hall breathed heavily in that suit as he kept up with me.

'What do you mean, your powers are gone? We need you to kill Pandora.'

'I'm not killing anyone for you, Hall.' I reached the sign and stopped. There was only one house on the side of the street, about a minute away. The mist was so thick, it was like someone was constructing a blue wall around us as we moved. 'We'll defeat Pandora using our wits.'

I ran towards the building as the demon laughed behind me.

'Good luck with that,' he said. I couldn't hear Claudia singing anymore.

Colleen and I reached the house together. She didn't ask me about my abilities, only putting her hand on mine.

'I've got your back.'

Hall and Allister didn't appear as we walked up the steps. I was about to knock when I realised how foolish that was. The blue was everywhere, seeping over our arms and legs. I pushed into the house before it covered us. Colleen slammed the door shut and I waited for the mist to drift underneath it or float down the stairs, but nothing came.

'You're safe in here; she's keeping it away from us.'

It was a man's voice coming from the living room. Colleen and I glanced at each other before striding along the corridor and turning into that room. It was large, bigger than any flat I'd ever lived in, but I ignored the furniture and décor and stared at the man near the far window. He looked familiar when he turned around, but I knew he wasn't President Dixon from the photos I'd seen. I didn't see anyone else, but was on my guard.

'Who are you?' I said.

'My name is Dexter, and you're the girl who kills presidents.'

I strode forward, with Colleen at my back scrutinising everything. 'Why do you look familiar?'

'You know my sister, Olivia Erasmus.' He moved from the window, and that's when the facial resemblance became obvious. They had the same eyes and cheekbones; even his hair was similar, if shorter. 'Do you want to say hello to her?'

'You have a phone which can call out of the Zone?'

He was two feet away from me when he tapped the side of his head.

'We communicate through this; she's told me all about you, Cassie.'

'You're both telepathic? What supernatural creatures are you?' Were they like me?

He shook his head. 'We can only converse with each other; we can't read other people's minds. And as far as I know, Olivia and I are human. We were born like this, grew up like this, and kept it quiet from everyone until now.'

Colleen stood at my side. 'I knew she was sneaky.'

'My sister has always been the strongest in our family. She was convinced you would come and save me.'

'Save you? What about the president?' Had the doctor tricked me all along?

'I don't think the former VP has a lot of friends in Washington. His politics are not authoritarian enough for the current political climate. Those who influence the government, such as big businesses, gun lobbyists, media giants, and the oil and gas barons, are looking for someone more hard-line than Dixon. You killed the man they put in the White House. I'm not sure many would miss Dixon at all.'

I dug my nails into my palms and drew blood. The thump of my heart must have been loud enough for both of them to hear it.

'Is he dead?'

'No.' He stepped past me. 'Follow me and I'll show you.'

He walked to the stairs and I looked at Colleen.

'We've come this far, Cassie; we might as well see it through.'

So we went up and followed Dexter Erasmus into the first bedroom. Lying on top of the bed was George Dixon, President of the United States.

'Once we saw what was happening to the town, when we witnessed what the blue mist did to the people, all we could do was retreat to this house. I think the mist infected him before we got inside and he's been like this ever since.'

I went to Dixon and peered into his vacant eyes. He was breathing, but there was no other sign of life. I'd stood over a coma victim before, my mother a lifetime ago, and recognised the signs.

I turned to Erasmus.

'This is what the blue mist does to people?' If that was so, where were they all?

He clutched at his chest. 'No, he's the only one it's happened to; of the ones I saw, anyway.'

Colleen stepped forward. 'What did you see?'

He sat on the bed, next to the slumbering president. The lines grew over his face and his eyes sank into his cheeks as he recounted his experience.

'We were outside with the security detail. At first, we believed it was an early morning fog. Dixon was getting ready for his daily jog when it crept forward and we saw the colour of it. Then we thought it could be from a fire. He got worried, not for himself, but for whoever might be in trouble. He told me to get on the phone. As I did that, someone, I don't know who, said it could be a chemical attack.'

He paused and steadied his breathing.

'What happened next?' I said.

'Then, before I could dial the first number, the blue mist changed into four long, swirling tendrils which shot into each of the security detail. I froze, my legs rooted to the spot as they lifted into the sky, with their bodies flailing in every direction.' He placed a hand over his face, but continued. 'I stood there and watched as that thing, whatever it is, sucked them dry.' He removed his fingers to wipe the tears from his cheeks.

'What do you mean?' I needed to know what Pandora was doing to people.

'All four of them shrivelled up as the blue consumed them like you or I would suck a milkshake through a straw; it took everything, even their clothes and weapons. I'd have been next if George hadn't pulled me into the house.' He looked at the president. 'He was in front of me, so I don't know how the mist got to him and not me. Or why he's like this and not devoured like the others.'

'That's because I always save some snacks for later.'

I turned too late to catch the owner of that voice before something crashed into the side of my head.

Before I knew what I was doing, my hands were around Lucy's throat as I pushed her to the floor.

'You lie!' I screamed at her.

There was no resistance as I continued to choke her. Was she powerless now, too weak to fight back? A red mist clouded my vision as Bella dragged me up and dumped me in the corner effortlessly.

'We need to remain calm, Alice.'

A combination of electricity and seething lava bubbled inside my veins. I refused Bella's hand and staggered to my feet, pointing trembling fingers at Lucy.

'She needs to explain herself.'

Bella helped Lucy up. 'She's right, my old friend.'

Lucy rubbed at her throat, but there were no marks there. Had I even done any damage? Was it all another deception, allowing me to pin her down like that?

'A lot has happened with your mother since you saw her last, Alice.'

The anger didn't subside. 'You mean since you stole her from that hospital bed the day she gave birth to Cassie and me? Or do you mean since the subsequent years you kept her imprisoned in Hell, before swapping her with Dracula for a piece of paper as if she was worthless?'

Her eyes shimmered red. 'Oh, your mother has never been worthless, Alice. And there's so much you don't know about her and the circumstances of your birth.'

I held out the palm of my hand and slammed it into the suit of armour close to me. It tumbled to the ground with a crash. A confused looking member of the Palace staff glanced in our direction and spoke to a colleague as he pointed at the mess on the floor.

I glared at Lucy. 'If you lie to me again, I won't stop until I've ripped your throat out next time.'

The two men strode towards the distressed suit of armour rolling at my feet.

Lucy looked at me. 'We need somewhere more private to continue this conversation.' She glanced down the corridor. 'Stay close to me, or the others will see you.'

She marched away from us. Angie followed first, then Bella. I had no choice but to go with them.

The First of the Fallen led us up a grand staircase, the four of us moving past groups of European Royalty mingling with politicians and celebrities. None of them looked in our direction and I wondered if they would, even if Lucy's cloak of invisibility didn't hide us. We were so far beneath them in the social strata, they probably would have thought we were servants; apart from Angie, who was still masquerading as a minor member of the Royal Family.

The bronze staircase glittered as we moved, with each part appearing to sparkle as Lucy went further. I peered at my reflection as we stepped up, gazing at this person who wasn't me, deliberating if I'd prefer to stay like this forever. Then I glanced at Bella without a reflection, unable to see herself. I wondered if she appeared in video or photos as I considered never seeing my real face again.

Bella seemed as confident as always, but looking at her, I'd considered for the first time what the reunion with Dracula would be like for Bella. I'd focused so much on my missing family, I'd never thought what this would do to her. And then there was Angie, cruelly taken from her mother and twin sister decades ago, before suffering the horrible experiments of one of the vilest regimes in history. There was so much family trauma between us, it was no wonder I felt a deep bond with them.

And there was Lucy. She'd tricked and betrayed me more than once, had lied and deceived me with virtually every word, but even she was struggling against her brother and a disappearing father. Against my better judgment, a tinge of sympathy was growing inside me for her, which should have been impossible. I touched a hand to my cheek as we continued following her, wondering if this new face had anything to do with my confusing thoughts.

Then I remembered what Lucy had done to Cassie and what she'd said about my mother, and the anger returned.

As I struggled to get it under control, the three of them stepped into a room and left the door open. I followed and closed it behind me, marching into a vast library overflowing with books. Lucy ignored them and headed for the sideboard and the alcohol.

'We should be okay in here for a bit.' She poured a glass of bourbon and the smell of it nearly knocked me out. 'Hopefully, it'll be long enough for us to come up with a plan to stop your mother ruining everything.'

I dug my nails into my palms and controlled my breathing. I hated strong spirits, but had to resist the temptation of having one. Angie and Bella had no such reservations, joining Lucy in partaking of the Royal booze. They looked like three women sipping drinks in the poshest wine bar ever, and it made my head spin. The anger and frustration rose in me like a cocktail.

'No more lies. Tell me everything you know about my mother, or I swear to God...'

Lucy flopped into the middle of a luxurious sofa, crossed her legs, and lifted the glass to her mouth. The bourbon glistened on her lips after she'd sipped at it.

'Ah God, that's where all this trouble started.'

The alcohol appeared to loosen Angie's inhibitions. 'What?'

'Well, the Creator refused to allow angels and humans to have relationships. So some of them did anyway, and we ended up with their offspring, the Nephilim, the thought of which so offended God, they sent the Great Flood to wipe the world clean, which was an overreaction if you ask me. But that didn't work and Alice's mother, the last surviving Nephilim, hid away for thousands of years. That's when her resentment at God grew and festered until she charmed an archangel into giving her a baby, which turned out to be two babies, so that she could have her revenge on the Creator. Now, with rumours of God's return to cleanse humans from the Earth, Mary Arcane wants to gather an army to battle what she hates the most.'

She was lying again. She had to be.

'My mother hid Cassie from you and Michael. So you're the ones dangerous to the world.'

Lucy raised the glass to me and shook her head.

'I'm sorry you had to find out this way, Alice, but it wasn't your mother who arranged your disappearance from the hospital, but your father.'

Nervous laughter burst from me. 'You can't help your-self, can you? Everything is a big lie for you.'

'Your father loved your mother, but he also feared her, never more so than when he found out what her plans were for her children. He promised to pass one child to me and one to Michael, but he changed his mind. When I got to the hospital, the two of you had been spirited away. I didn't see you until you took your little trip through time.'

She placed one lie on top of another like falling dominoes. But maybe there was still an opportunity for me to discover some truth from her.

'What happened to my father?'

'Heaven's angels apprehended him not long after he secreted you and Cassie away. He never revealed your whereabouts because I'm sure he didn't know where you were.'

The blade was in my hand as I stomped towards her. 'I told you what would happen if you lied to me again.'

She sipped at the alcohol. 'Why would I lie to you, Alice?'

Nervous laughter jumped out of me. 'You're the Queen of Lies, the Duchess of Deception. Everything you say and do is a mistruth. You lie because it's second nature to you, but I think you're doing this just to annoy me.' I pushed the blade at her face.

There was no fear in her eyes. 'If you don't believe me, then you should ask your mother.'

Lucy pointed at the door as it opened. Dracula strode through first, followed by her: Mary Arcane, my mother.

'Well, this is awkward.' Dracula glanced at Bella, and then at me.

I dropped the knife to the floor. My mother walked towards me and placed her fingers on my cheek.

'I'd know my Alice anywhere.' The tears in her eyes reflected mine. 'It's been so long.'

She lowered her hand and thrust her arms around me. My fingers shook as I wrapped them around her waist; my legs trembled and I was ready to drop. After an age, we separated and fell silent in each other's gaze.

Dracula appeared unhappy at this unexpected family reunion.

'What are you doing here, Isabella?'

Bella circled him, her eyes never leaving his.

'Alice needed my help in untangling her mother from your clutches, Brother.'

A shrill erupted from the Lord of the Vampires as he clutched at his chest.

'Oh, Sister, you were never one to grasp the truth in front of you, were you?'

I wiped the tears from my face and grabbed the blade from the floor.

'You traded the contract protecting your life for my mother's servitude from Lucy. We know this. Your lies won't change that.'

Dracula scratched at his chin. 'That may have been true at the start, but it didn't take long for Mary and me to fall in love. Our relationship is equal now.'

I watched my mother as he spoke; her eyes sparkled at the sound of his voice. I took her hand.

'Is this true?'

She smiled at me. 'You never know when love will strike, Alice, even in the strangest of circumstances.'

Bella laughed. 'It's Stockholm Syndrome.'

'Why are you in the Palace?' Lucy said.

Dracula moved to my mother and embraced her fingers in his. The sight made my stomach churn.

'It's always polite to take your prospective bride to meet your relations.'

My legs finally gave way as my knees buckled and I stumbled into a table, sending the Royals' best china crashing to the floor. It was only Angie's capable grasp which stopped me from joining the cups and saucers. As she lifted me, the miraculous changes she'd applied to my face came unstuck. My skin rippled against my bones, an unpleasant feeling similar to having your head pushed up against a water stream.

I glanced at my reflection in the mirror, the resemblance to my mother not making me feel any better.

'This can't be true. You can't be in love with him.' I struggled to catch my breath. 'He's a vampire, a monster.'

The woman I'd done so much to find peered at me through cold eyes.

'You need to be an adult now, Alice. I've been on my own for so long since your father betrayed and abandoned me.' She pointed at Lucy. 'And she abducted me and kept me captive for sixteen years.'

It was my turn to point. 'And she sold you into slavery to him.' I spat the words at Dracula.

My mother shrugged. 'Cupid's arrow is strange and unpredictable.'

'You're lying,' Lucy said. 'And as an expert in deception, I should know. You're here to reveal some minor Royal as a werewolf to the human world.' She peered straight at my mother. 'You are the Creator of Chaos, Mary Arcane. You should be truthful with your daughter.'

My mother bent over with laughter. When she straightened up, her face was flushed red.

'Oh my, how rich that is from the Queen of Lies. Why would I want to do such a thing?'

I stepped towards her. 'Lucy claims you only had Cassie and me as part of some grand revenge plan against God for trying to kill you, and it was our father who hid us, away from you as much as the archangels.'

She grinned at me. 'That's nonsense, Alice. Why would you believe her after she's lied to you so many times and after she betrayed you and abandoned Cassie?'

She was right. None of what Lucy had said made any sense. And she could never be trusted. I turned to the Morningstar, ready to decry her deception when the room exploded and everything went dark.

26 CASSIE: PANDORA

I woke downstairs, slumped on the sofa with Colleen in a chair opposite me. She was still out cold, but neither of us was trussed or tied up. The lump on my head throbbed like a disco ball and I smelt ice cream. My neck hurt as I twisted to the side, staring at Dexter Erasmus sitting at the living room table. Next to him was a woman slurping on a tub of chocolate chip Ben and Jerry's.

'Humans make the best food.' She winked at me. 'In more ways than one.' I flexed my leg and felt something at my feet. When I looked down, I saw it was an empty hazmat suit. 'That wasn't a good starter; he was too chewy and so tasteless. Still, it was enough to get me beyond the barrier and into this dimension.' She held the ice cream as she left the table and sat next to Colleen. Erasmus's hands shook and his face twitched as he stared at me.

I peered at her. 'Are you Pandora?'

Her dark eyes matched her hair, a stronger shade of purple than the dress she wore. She placed the tub on Colleen's leg and removed a jar from inside the dress.

'I like your clothes, Cassie; they seem much more practical than this old thing I'm wearing. I must wander into town and get me some.' She held out her hand to me. 'Do you want a sweet?'

Pandora opened the jar and took something from it, placing it between her fingers and pushing it towards me: it was a human eye. I tried to move forward, but there was lead in my body.

'Who did you kill?'

She sucked in her cheeks and narrowed her eyes. 'What, since I returned to this world? Do you want me to name all four thousand or so of them? Or just the one near your legs?'

'Was it Hall?'

Pandora took the ice cream from the top of Colleen's leg and dropped the eyeball into it. Then she dug her fingers inside and scooped everything together.

'Yes, I think that was his name: Hall, or Ball, or Fall; there's been so many of them it's hard to keep up. Especially when I was still in the other dimension, or at least my mind was.' She crossed her legs and sighed. 'But that's all behind me, literally, and now I've got the new life promised to me.'

'Promised by whom?'

I had to keep her talking. Once before, I'd been frozen like this when Alice and I had travelled through time to find our mother and stumbled into an archangel war. I'd only escaped then because Alice had somehow tapped into our Arcane abilities. I had to do the same while Pandora rattled on. If she'd been stuck in another dimension for thousands of years, she was probably desperate to talk to anybody.

'It doesn't matter who poked a hole in that prison wall, but the humans are to blame, really; if they hadn't weakened the planet's natural climate, it would have been impossible for me to sneak back here, regardless of who helped me.'

Inside my head, I pictured every sinew and bone flexing against the unseen force confining me. My memory returned to Lucy's lessons, teaching me to fly, teleport, turn invisible, move things with my mind, and read others' thoughts. I strained and strained, but the only thing which happened was I started to sweat.

'You and I are related.'

She put the tub back on Colleen's leg. 'Yes, I was told that; how fascinating it is.' She leant towards me. 'That's why I removed the explosive from your neck and got rid of it. I can't have a family member going kaboom when we've only just met.' Pandora pointed at me. 'There, I've released your arms so you can check your throat.'

I did that, touching my skin and feeling nothing underneath it. 'How did you do that?'

'Oh, it was simple. I did it for all of your little friends as well, even though I know you came here to kill me.'

I gazed at Colleen's neck. 'You removed the bombs inside all of them?'

She flexed her fingers and grinned at me. 'I can't have my food exploding on me, can I? That would be a case of the worst jelly belly ever.'

As she continued to smirk, I noticed a slight movement in Colleen's eyes. Maybe if Pandora focused on me, her grip on the banshee would slip away.

'You don't have to kill anyone, Pandora; you can exist peacefully in this world.'

She grabbed the tub again, scooped out its contents, and gulped them down.

'I call this my eye cream. I suppose the humans would say it's soul food.'

'I can show you how to live with them.'

Pandora shook her head. 'It's too late for that, Cassie Arcane. First, they betrayed me and blamed me for everything; then they tricked me into stepping into that other realm and left me there.' She threw the tub over the hazmat suit. 'Do you know what it was like in that place? Do you?' Rage consumed her, with eyes a fiery red, while every part of her face undulated and shimmered.

'No, I don't. But I was abandoned and alone, separated from my mother and sister. So I understand what it's like to be isolated.'

She spat ice cream and eyeball over the floor. 'It's not the same. There was nothing in that place, only darkness. These..., these humans imprisoned me in there for eternity. I will eat every one of them, and then you and I and those like us shall inherit the Earth.' Steam came out of her ears, her nostrils flaring as her eyes grew as wide as her head. Her focus must have gone as Colleen's eyes blinked open.

And so did her mouth.

She turned to Pandora and screamed a second after I had my hands over my ears. Pandora was thrown across the table, crashing against the far wall and taking Erasmus with her. I was out of my seat as a thousand bells rang inside my head. I ignored the pain and grabbed Colleen. She said something to me, but I couldn't hear it, so I shouted at her.

'Get to the others.'

Then my hearing popped into life as she spoke. 'What about the president?'

'I need to deal with Pandora first.'

Colleen opened the door and outside there was no more blue, no more mist. Whatever she'd done to Pandora, it had affected the town. I was about to turn back when something grabbed me and threw me through the window.

I crashed through it, taking wood and glass with me. My shoulder smashed into the ground, concrete slicing into me and adding to my face and head cuts. I rolled with the momentum, pain surging through every sinew as I peered up to see Colleen sprinting down the road. I twisted to my side and watched Pandora striding towards me. If I needed my Arcane abilities, it was now.

But they didn't come.

I looked around for a weapon, but found nothing. Then I remembered the pen in my pocket. My hand was on it as she spoke.

'Family or not, you will die. I don't care about the promise I made. You will die.' Blood covered her face, bits of flesh dripping from her cheeks and forehead. 'And then I'll slaughter every one of your friends, starting with that Irish witch.'

She grabbed me from the floor and lifted me, pulling me close to her injured head. There was nothing in her eyes but burning fire. Her fingers dug into my shoulders, cutting into me like acid, and I dropped the pen. As I screamed, I buried my face in hers and bit deep. I tore chunks from her, drank on her blood and pulled out her flesh. Pandora threw me to the ground and howled. I wiped her blood across my lips, tasting it again, and it was sweet like honey.

'I gave you your chance, Pandora. Tell me who helped you, and I'll let you live.'

A growl escaped from her as she pushed up to her full height. The blue fog, which had vanished, reappeared behind her, swirling and twisting like a tornado.

'You stupid, stupid girl. I'll find your sister and mother and kill them too.'

She lifted her hands and the haze gathered around her arms. It crawled over her shoulders and head before engulfing every part of her. For one second, I believed she'd consumed herself, and then she threw her hand out and the blue shot into me: it pressed inside me, slithering through my veins and biting at my muscle and bone. It pounced into my heart and smothered my brain. I couldn't breathe. I couldn't move. I dropped to the ground and pushed my palms into the concrete. This was my end, and all I thought of was Alice.

Alice, I let you down.

Alice, I wasn't good enough for you.

Alice, I miss you.

As I expected my last breath, I rose; I was flying.

My head twisted around to stare at Pandora.

This can't be happening. The girl should be dead.

I was inside her head, reading her mind. I was the Arcane again. My legs strengthened and I moved forward. I pushed out my chest, and the blue mist shot out of me. She prepared to attack once more, but I disappeared.

I teleported behind her and got my arms around her neck.

'Who helped you, Pandora? Who facilitated your journey here?'

She struggled in my grip, but there was no way out for her. But how long would it last? My Arcane abilities had returned just like they'd vanished; they could go as quickly as they'd come. I had to deal with her without delay. I loosened my hold so she could talk.

'I'll never tell you, child. So you might as well kill me now, because if you don't, I'll unleash holy Hell on the entire planet.'

I increased my grip on her until she slipped into unconsciousness. She lay limp in my arms, but she was right. There was only one thing I could do.

I teleported to the others, dropping between Claudia and Colleen. I held on to Pandora as they stared at me.

'Is she dead?' Claudia said.

I shook my head. 'She's sleeping for now, but I don't know how long she'll stay like that, so we haven't much time.' I spoke to Wovoka. 'Did you find what we need?'

He nodded. 'I did.' There was a small jar in his hands. 'I brought this from the spirit realm.'

'Is that what I think it is?'

'It's the original jar which contained all the evils of the world. This is what was used to send Pandora to the Abyss.'

Pandora squirmed in my arms as she jolted awake. 'No, no,' she screamed. 'I will not return to that place.' She twisted her head to me. 'I'd rather you killed me than leave me there.' She fought against my hold and I was slipping. My abilities were waning. This had to be done now.

'What do we need to send her through, Wovoka?'

'Only one thing, Cassandra Kane. She was born from angel blood, and only that can banish her.'

'Great,' Colleen said. 'And where do we find one of those around here?'

I threw Pandora to the floor and put my foot on her back. She struggled against it, but I had enough strength left to keep her down; but for how long?

'Bring the jar over here,' I said.

Wovoka did so and I placed my wrist over it. With my other hand, I took my longest nail and cut across my flesh. Then we all watched the blood drip into the container.

'What are you doing?' Luke said.

'My name is Cassandra Arcane, a child of the Nephilim. Part of my heritage is the blood of an archangel.' My hand ached as my life dripped into the jar. 'Let's hope this is enough to send her back.'

Once it was full, I pulled away, trying not to look at the horror in Luke's eyes.

'Let me fix that,' Claudia said as she tied one of her socks around my wrist.

'What happens now?' I said. Pandora was getting stronger as I became weaker.

'Smash the jar on the floor,' Wovoka said. 'And that should do it.'

I didn't question what he said, about to throw the jar to the ground when Pandora slipped from under my foot. She leapt to her feet and I stumbled back, still clinging to the jar.

'Fools, that will never work. You need the essence of a pure-blood angel to banish me.' She glared at me. 'Not the muck from some half-breed.'

The fire burnt inside her eyes as the blue mist returned. We all watched as it gathered above her head like a tornado. Then thick tendrils of it shot out of her and pierced every one of us.

The others screamed as Pandora lifted us all into the air like a demented octopus toying with its prey. Pain rushed through me as I stared at the agony on Claudia's face. My fingers clutched the jar as more blue mist slithered towards my hand and the container of my blood.

As Pandora tried to take it from me, I used my last strength to hurl the jar to the ground. The glass smashed into a hundred pieces and my blood sank into the concrete.

Silence invaded the air as Pandora stood still. Her eyes shrank into her face as the mist swirled around her like a manic tornado.

But then it shimmered and disappeared, and we all dropped to the ground. Pandora peered at her hands as I looked on in fascination. The pieces of the jar vibrated at my feet as Pandora became fainter and fainter. She opened her mouth to say something or to scream, her eyes burning into me, and then she vanished.

The jar reassembled itself and I picked it up.

'Who wants this for safekeeping?'

Allister reached for it, but I sidestepped him. I hadn't seen him reappear and was sure he hadn't been lifted into the air like the rest of us. Wovoka took the jar from me as the demon held up his hands.

'Okay, okay; I deserved that. I guess we better get the president now,' he said.

As he smiled at me, I thumped him straight in the face, using all the Arcane strength I had left. He crumpled to the ground in a heap.

I felt like doing the same.

Claudia burst out laughing. 'Excellent. I'm glad you did that, but why did you do that?'

I flexed my knuckles to exorcise the pain. 'Because that's no demon.'

Colleen puffed on a cigarette through an enormous smile. 'So, who is he?'

A sliver of blood dripped from Claudia's sock to the ground.

'That's the Archangel Michael.'

27 ALICE: THE CURSE

A violent ringing filled my ears and my skull throbbed as if it was inside a microwave. Someone was on top of me. Dust and debris swirled everywhere, invading my lungs and instigating a nasty cough that forced me up. Angie leant against me, a wound in her shoulder and blood over her chest. Her eyes were dazed and confused.

I gripped her fingers. 'Are you okay?'

The sound of conflict drowned out my voice, but she must have heard me.

'I'll live. What happened?'

I pushed us against the far wall, my legs buckling under the stress. A group of armed security guards had Lucy pinned to the floor. Bits of plaster fell on me as I twisted my head towards the ceiling. High above, swaying back and forth between the expensive crystal chandeliers, Bella and Dracula floated in the air with their hands around each other's throats. Smoke drifted across my face as I searched for Mary and found nothing.

I pulled Angie closer. 'We need to get out of here.'

'I agree, but how?'

Books were scattered over the floor as I led her from the wall. I wanted to shout for my mother, but it was useless in this cacophony of yelling and violence. As we crept through the damage, I glanced up to see the two vampires rolling across the ceiling and destroying everything in their wake; glass and plaster rained down on us in a painful fashion. Angie and I stumbled behind a large sofa for protection.

Lucy and her attackers were between us and the door. It was open and I hoped my mother had escaped from this carnage. I gave no thought to Lucy's claims or what Mary had said about being in love with Dracula. He must have enchanted her somehow, so all I had to do was get her away from him to break that spell.

As long as I could find her again.

I let go of Angie. The only way out of the room was through the armed men. I was reaching over to grab the nearest bloke when he turned and threw a punch at me. Angie pushed me to the side and his fist connected with her cheek. She went tumbling into the wall, her face changing from fake royalty into the real Angie as she slumped to the floor.

He was moving to hit her again before I jumped on him. My arms were around his neck, pulling him back as I dug my nails into his cheeks. Even with the other noises howling in the room, I heard his shriek as he threw both of us into the nearest table.

I hit it first, scattering ornaments everywhere as I fell, and he landed on top of me. Now it was his fingers at my throat, squeezing hard as I fought to push him off. I tried to get my knee into his gut, but he was too heavy. Then, as I struggled in vain, something dragged him from me.

As I reached for Angie, my arms shook as I was glad to see she was okay and standing against the wall. As she helped me up, we both surveyed the carnage in the room, shocked to see what was happening to our attackers. The whole group, four of them, had been lifted into the air and hung there like butterflies caught inside a typhoon.

Lucy stood with her arms pointed up, not looking at us and grinning at the men as they aimed their weapons at her.

Now was our chance to flee. I grabbed Angie and pulled her forward as the blast of gunfire shattered the space before me; four floating automatic rifles spat toxic metal deep into Lucy's chest. The clatter of bullets breaking through flesh and bone assaulted my ears. A red mist drifted out of Lucy and hovered between her and the security. She lifted her hands towards them, seemingly untroubled by the ammunition emptied into her. Then, with the flick of her fingers, she tore each of the guards apart. Arms and legs flew into the walls, torsos collapsing under her powers as guts and entrails dropped onto the carpet. Above all that red were the decapitated heads she was toying with. I peered at them in horror, seeing the movement behind their eyes.

I was transfixed by revulsion until a hand grabbed my arm and pulled me away.

'Now she's possessed by the bloodlust and she'll kill us all.' My mother spoke through a swirl of dirt. 'We won't get past her to escape.'

I wiped the dust from my face. 'I don't think she'll hurt me.'

Lucy juggled the heads above her as the blood stained her clothes.

Mary Arcane took my hands. 'I'm not sure about that, Alice, but she won't allow me out of here alive.'

I gazed deep into her eyes and knew it was the truth. All the lies Lucy had spouted couldn't hide the hate she had for my mother. It wasn't just God who loathed the Nephilim.

'Don't worry; I know what to do.'

I let go of Mary's hands and strode towards Lucy. The Morningstar stood there, giggling like a schoolkid as she flew those heads around the room.

Then she noticed me.

'What do you think, Alice? Should I use these as cannonballs and aim them at those two useless vampires rolling across the ceiling?'

I peered up to where Bella and her brother continued to grapple with each other. A pang of guilt struck me in the chest when I stared at Bella with the realisation of what I was about to do.

I held my hand out to Lucy.

'You can leave them with their family squabbles because we've got more important things to discuss.'

Lucy gazed at me in surprise, her eyes large and shimmering. She took my fingers and gripped them. I dragged her to me so she fell into my chest. We were pressed together like long-lost lovers, her blood staining my clothes until I pulled away from her touch. She glanced over my shoulder at Angie and my mother.

'You won't like what I'm about to say, Alice.'

I pointed at her wounds. 'Doesn't that hurt?'

Lucy rubbed her fingers. 'It stings a little, that's all.' She removed a piece of plaster from her hair. 'What I told you about your mother earlier is all true. She wants to use you and your sister in a war against God's followers, and she won't care how many humans die in the crossfire or what happens to this planet.' As she paused, all four decapitated heads fell to the floor and rolled around my feet.

'You abducted her from the hospital and kept her captive for sixteen years; why didn't you do something about her then?'

She shrugged. 'She was under my control then. Of course, you and Cassie were always more important than her, but I knew she could be a bargaining chip one day.'

'This is what you did with Dracula to get that contract Cassie and I signed promising not to kill the bearer.'

Lucy kicked a head across the room. 'I did, and it's an agreement I still have in my possession, remember? You can't stop me from killing your mother.'

'I always keep my word, but you must promise me one thing.'

Her eyes sparkled and gleamed like shooting stars. 'And what would that be, Alice Arcane?'

'I have to be the one to do it.'

Light beamed out of her. 'Excellent; I'll make a protégé out of you yet.' She rubbed her hands again. 'You need to kill the Nazi shapeshifter as well; she's quite the abomination.'

I didn't reply, only turning to walk towards Angie and my mother.

'We heard everything,' Mary said.

I smiled at them before pressing my fingers into the dark stains on my chest. Then I placed my arms around both of their shoulders and pulled them to me. I squeezed them as tight as I could.

Then I drank the Devil's blood from my fingertips.

Lucy screamed as we disappeared, my heart full of guilt at leaving Bella behind.

We reappeared at King's Cross train station. I let go of them and dropped to my knees. There was no pain this time, only a sense of ecstatic euphoria as if the whole of me flowed with joy. My senses were heightened, hearing every heartbeat around me, tasting the air in my lungs, smelling the aroma of freshly baked pastries and cakes on the stalls outside the entrance to the station. People stared at us, and then moved on as if we were just another sideshow in the nation's capital.

Angie lifted me. 'How did you do that?'

Some of Lucy's blood continued to linger on my hands as I peered at them.

'I had some unexpected help.'

'We can't stay here,' my mother said. 'The Morningstar will find us if we dawdle too long; her spies are everywhere.'

Angie reached into her pocket and got two credit cards. She gave one to me and one to my mother.

'Take these and get a train to wherever you want.'

'What will you do?' I said.

Angie placed her fingers over her face as her flesh shimmered behind them. When she removed them, I stared into a mirror.

'I'll be you for a few hours and lead your pursuers away. Then, I'll take them deep into the supernatural underground where I have many friends, many dangerous friends. I'll be fine; now go.' She pointed at the entrance to the train station.

My mother didn't need a second invitation. She grabbed my hand and pulled us towards the sounds of incoming trains. I shot Angie a last look, mouthed goodbye and thanked her.

We were on the way to the ticket office and peering at the electronic board full of arrivals and departures before I could say anything. I glanced at the credit card Angie had given me.

'Where shall we go?'

Mother took the card from me. 'I have people and resources in the north. We should be safe there for a while.'

A whirlwind of emotions possessed me: I was relieved

to be out of Buckingham Palace, happy to be reunited with my mother, but also confused about what she'd said, and haunted by a continuous burning ache from being away from Cassie.

She must have recognised the anguish inside my eyes.

'Don't worry; we'll rescue your sister once we're safe and I'm with my people.' Before I could reply, she was at the front of the queue and had bought two tickets for the next train to Leeds. 'I got First Class as they provide free food and drink, and I'm sure we could both do with that.'

I followed her through the crowd of customers. She thrust a ticket into my hand and pointed to the details on the giant board. There was a train leaving in ten minutes from platform six. The journey would take about two-and-a-half hours. Plenty of time for questions, but I was already impatient.

We pressed our tickets against the electronic scanners on the gates and made our way to First Class. I was by her side as I spoke.

'What do you mean when you say reunited with your people?'

She ignored the question and got on the train. I stepped behind her and into the carriage. We had comfortable looking table seats, next to the window and opposite each other.

My mother stared at me.

'Are you keeping Lucy's blood for later, or will you get cleaned up?'

I looked at my hands, and then my clothes, smelling the Devil's stain all over me. A nagging desire nibbled at the back of my brain.

Drink some more; you know you want to. It's manna

from Heaven, the food of the gods. Think of all the wonderful things you can do with just a taste of it.

The train rumbled out on the tracks as I held my fingers in front of my face. I bent them into claws and dug my nails into the palms of my hands. I peered at my mother, suddenly fearful she would abandon me again.

'If I get cleaned up, will you still be here when I return?'

Her smile was warmer than the sun.

'I will, Alice. We have so much to talk about, haven't we?'

My legs trembled as I stood and went to the toilets. Once I was inside, the movement of the train synchronised with the velocity of my churning guts. I turned the tap on and stared into the mirror, gazing into the face I'd never been comfortable with, seeing not only me, but also Cassie and my mother. The liquid was warm as I washed Lucy's blood from my hands and my clothes.

The first stage was done: I'd found my mother after all this time.

Now together, we'd rescue Cassie.

As the water turned red, I knew nothing could stop me.

M y knuckles were turning into a delicate shade of purple as I flexed them. Colleen was bent over Allister and dragging on a cigarette.

'This is the Archangel Michael? How do you know?'

I pulled dead skin from my hand. 'There was something about him I recognised at the prison. I thought it was the demon possession I'd seen before, but an itch kept irritating the back of my head as soon as we got on the plane.' I focused on him as he lay on the ground. 'And then I couldn't understand why he didn't flee that body.' I glanced at Brooks and Cave. 'I know Hall claimed Section 25 had discovered a way to prevent demon possession in humans, but I wasn't convinced. Plus, even with that, he had chances to leave us when we were in the forest, and I threw away the explosive trigger, but he continued hanging around and coming back. None of it made sense to me, but I was too preoccupied with Pandora to think about it. Then Pandora said something in the house and it all clicked.'

Claudia was at my side. 'What did she say?'

'She bragged about someone helping her break out of

her prison and how she wouldn't keep a promise not to hurt me. Even when she'd frozen me to the sofa, I wondered who she meant. Apart from Alice and my mother, only the two archangels cared about what happened to me; Lucy and Michael.'

Claudia thumped me on the arm. 'Hey!'

I rubbed where she'd hit me and smiled at her. 'Sorry. And you, of course, but that's when I realised Allister wasn't a demon and had to be an archangel.' I stared down at him. 'I knew it couldn't be Lucy. I've been inside her mind and tasted her blood: I'd recognise her anywhere. So it had to be Michael.'

'But why the deception?' Luke said.

'I can only think it's for one of two things.' I glanced down the road, now free of blue mist. 'Michael controlled the previous American president and the British prime minister to start a nuclear apocalypse, so maybe he wants to do the same with Dixon. The other option is his obsession with me.' Was it vain to believe this was all about me? I guess Colleen thought so too.

She flicked her cigarette to the ground.

'Don't get me wrong, Cassie, you're a great kid and all, but why would an archangel go to all this trouble for you?'

I didn't just look at her, but all of them: should I let them know about Michael's claim of God returning to wipe the Earth clean of all life? And that Lucy and Michael wanted to use Alice and me for their own ends when God arrived? I thought it probably wasn't a good idea, and they had to leave before Michael woke up.

'I'm just special, I suppose.' I put my hand on Colleen's arm. 'You need to get everyone into the Dixon house. Tell Dexter Erasmus to contact his sister for Section 25 to send a recovery team here as soon as possible.'

'And what will you do?'

I peered at the fallen demon. 'If this is Michael, I have to deal with him.'

'How?' Luke said. 'Do you still have your powers?'

I held out my fingers. 'No, they've gone. I'm unsure why they come and go like this, but I'm a normal girl again.'

Claudia took my hand. 'You'll never be a normal girl, Cassie Arcane. And I'm not leaving you alone with him. I don't care if he's a demon, archangel, or the Easter Bunny.'

Luke grabbed my other hand. 'None of us will abandon you.'

I wriggled free from them both. 'You have to. You don't know what Michael is like. He'll kill you all to get to me. If I promise to leave with him, then he'll spare everyone.' As I spoke, he moved on the ground. 'We haven't got much time. You have to go to the house now.'

'There's no need to sacrifice yourself, Cassandra Arcane.' Wovoka stepped forward. 'I know what needs to be done with the archangel.'

'What do you mean?'

'I will take him into the spirit worlds and away from here.'

Claudia scratched at her chin. 'I thought there was only Heaven or Hell after this life?' She winked at me. 'I guess it'll be hot where I'm going.'

'Not for a long time,' I said. 'But there's more than that to the afterlife; there's Limbo and Purgatory as well. I've been to both places and they're not pleasant.' And that was putting it mildly.

'There are more realms than that, Cassie, both of the living and the dead.' Wovoka stood over Allister. 'The spirit worlds are endless.' He peered at Claudia. 'The one you pass through before reaching your final destination depends on many things: the life you've lived, the good or harm you've done, and even when and how you die. A violent death will send you to one of the worst places.' He looked at all of us. 'So avoid that if you can.'

Colleen lit another cigarette. 'That's what I've been trying to do all my life, mate.'

Wovoka handed me Pandora's jar. 'This won't be safe with me where I'm taking the archangel.'

'What will you do?'

'I'll drag him down through many realms. By the time he gets free, you'll be gone from here. But I'll only be able to contain him for so long, so whatever you do, be quick.'

Sayan put her hand on his arm. 'They'll have more time if we do this together.' The medicine man and the shamanka embraced, and then pulled apart without another word to each other. Then Sayan turned to me. 'This will get you home, Cassandra Arcane.'

I took a yellow flower from her. 'What do I do with this?' It fluttered in my hand and smelt of lemonade.

'Place a drop of your blood in the centre of the petals. It will seep into the flower, then bring it to your face and inhale its aroma. It will transport you from here.'

'Transport me where?'

'Blood finds blood, Child of the Nephilim. It will take you to your blood, to your sister.'

I looked at Claudia. 'I can't leave people behind.'

Claudia grabbed my hand. 'You're only going across the water. I'll be on a plane to England later today. I'll find you over there, don't you worry.'

Allister mumbled on the floor.

'We have to go,' Sayan said.

She and Wovoka took a demon arm each. There was no singing or dancing this time, and I guessed this was because they weren't searching for specific spirits. Then they whispered something I didn't hear and the three of them faded into nothing.

I turned to the others to say my goodbyes.

'Colleen, ensure you tell Olivia Erasmus what happened here. She has to know the supernatural is not all terrible monsters; we can also help this world.' And now I knew this. 'And keep this safe.' I handed her Pandora's jar. Then we shook hands, and I nodded my thanks to Brooks and Cave. I hugged Luke and it was a long embrace.

'I'll see you again, British girl; that's a Harlem promise.'

'Maybe I'll visit you there one day; give you a hand keeping those streets clean. I'm good with a brush.'

He laughed. 'I bet you are.'

Then there was Claudia. 'I won't cry,' she said. 'Because this isn't goodbye.' I saw the tear in her eye. 'I'll put those Brits right before you can say cream tea and scones.' She grinned at me. 'You know, I kissed David Bowie once. Well, it may have been more than once and possibly more than a kiss, but I'll tell you that story when we're reunited on English soil.'

I kept on laughing as I removed her sock from my wrist and squeezed a drop of blood into the flower. Then I waited for it to be absorbed while the others watched. After a minute, I lifted it to my face and breathed in. It smelt of the summer as a flock of pigeons flew into the town. I smiled to see they were only ordinary birds.

Blood goes to blood.

And I thought of Alice.

Then I disappeared.

And then reappeared with a thump, backside into hard concrete and my shoulder hitting a wall. A dull, throbbing ache sped through my legs and didn't stop until it got to my head. I peered at the stone above me, with damp and bits of grass hanging from the walls. I'd landed in some dirty room stinking of unwashed bodies and rotten food. How had Alice ended up here?

I pushed my fingers into the wall, finding dirt and insects crawling there; it was wet to the touch as I snatched my hand away. The air was full of dust, and I thought of Luke and Claudia and Colleen and what I'd left behind. But I'd come here for Alice.

Blood goes to blood.

But where was she and what was this place? It was small, no bigger than the last one-room bedsit I'd lived in. There were no windows or anywhere for light to enter or any sign of a door. The only illumination came from the few flickering candles opposite me.

Then, I realised something else was there. It appeared to be a formless shape glued to the far wall, maybe an outcrop of nature from the ancient stone.

Until it moved.

He shifted, his head inching away from the damp and the dirt. His body was withered and bony, encased in clothes that were nothing but rags. A thick grey beard obscured most of his face apart from the crisscrossing of scars underneath his eyes, pale blue ones appearing like dim lights as he stared at me. He stumbled forward, dust and grime swirling in the air because of his movement and making me cough. The chain around his ankle stopped him from reaching me. I pushed my spine into the wall, fingers clawing at the stone that cut into my nails. Coming from him was the smell of something which had died, then had been resurrected, and later died again.

'I knew this would happen one day, but I hoped it wouldn't be like this.' His voice was raspy and guttural, a spark returning to his eyes. 'You should leave before they come.'

Before I could reply, wailing and screaming filled the air, sounds sending daggers through my heart.

'What is that noise?'

'That's the chorus of the damned.' A trembling bony hand reached out to me. 'Are you Cassandra or Alice?'

'I'm Cassie.' Had Sayan's magic flower not worked? Blood goes to blood, she'd said. Was Alice in a British jail for what she'd done with the prime minister? Or was this where Lucy had imprisoned my mother? It had to be a prison cell. 'Who are you, and where am I?'

He held out his trembling arms. 'This is The Devastation and I'm Gabriel, father to Alice and Cassandra Arcane.'

I stumbled to the side, my hand hitting the far wall. His words bounced around my head as my eyes darted everywhere but on him. Then, finally, my vision adjusted to the gloom, glancing over the four walls, the floor and the ceiling: there was no way out; no window, door or exit.

Blood will find blood.

THANK YOU!

Thank you, dear reader for purchasing this book.

If you enjoyed reading about Alice and Cassie Arcane their journey continues in these books:

The Arcane Supernatural Thriller Series
Book one: The Arcane
Book two: The Arcane Identity
Book three: The Arcane Quest
Book four: The Arcane Ultimatum

Many thanks to my wonderful wife for all her support and patience.

My eternal gratitude to Wendy Cross for being the first person to read the Arcane and who gave me essential feedback on the characters and the plot.

Extra special thanks to Karina Gallagher for being a dedicated reader of my work.

The Arcane Quest edited by Alison Jack.

Cover design by James, GoOnWrite.com

ABOUT THE AUTHOR

Andrew French lives amongst faded seaside glamour on the North East coast of England. He likes gin and cats but not together, new music and old movies, curry and ice cream. Slow bike rides and long walks to the pub are his usual exercise, as well as flicking through the pages of good books and the memoirs of bad people.

Find out more at www.andrewsfrench.com

Facebook:

https://www.facebook.com/A-S-French-Author-150145625006018

Twitter:

www.twitter.com/andrewfrench100

Instagram:

www.instagram.com/andrewfrench100

And replies to all his email at mail@andrewsfrench.com

If you have the time, please leave a review at Amazon or Goodreads

Thank you!